Kill That Deputy

Deputy Sheriff Rod Kane was in deep trouble for he had been forced to kill the hellion Clay Latimer, the brother of the woman Rod loved. Worse still the notorious gunslinger Gideon James was supposedly in town and a warrant was out for his arrest. Then it looked as if the missing sheriff had been murdered.

Rod started out on the trail of the sidewinders but it wasn't long before he was captured, strung up over a fire and left to die. It surely looked as if the deputy would soon see his Maker, but he wasn't an easy man to kill.

Now it was the turn of the murderers to watch out for Rod had vengeance in his heart and guns in his hands.

Kill That Deputy

LEE BAXTER

A Black Horse Western

ROBERT HALE · LONDON

© 1971, 2002 Norman Lazenby.
First hardcover edition 2002
Originally published in paperback as
Kill That Deputy by Wes Yancey

ISBN 0 7090 7191 4

Robert Hale Limited
Clerkenwell House
Clerkenwell Green
London EC1R 0HT

Typeset by
Derek Doyle & Associates, Liverpool.
Printed and bound in Great Britain by
Antony Rowe Limited, Wiltshire.

1

Shamefaced Deputy

He came up out of the arid lands on horseback, a slow trip that had taken him three days on a plodding animal as tired as he was. His stetson was thick with desert dust, and around his neck sweat had caked the dust into something like a mud pack. His red bandana reeked of salt perspiration; his brown pants tucked into once-black riding boots, smelled of warm horse-flesh.

Occasionally he glanced back at a second horse he led on a rope, and at the dead hulk of the corpse the animal carried.

Clay Latimer was real dead – a fate he had begged for, it seemed, in his wild hellion manner of living. Only his sister, June would mourn him in Cactus Plain, unless one of his pals decided to resent his way of dying – and the man who had killed him.

Rod Kane squinted into the heat haze, at the dancing little mirages that topped every distant sandy rise. He had been forced into killing Latimer in a shoot-up that had to spell death for one of them, a fracas that had come at the end of a grim four-day trail into the badlands.

Maybe June would understand, if only he could talk to her first before someone else found enjoyment in throwing the brutal news at her. He would have to talk to the girl – but not with a limp body with a hole in its head folded over the saddle. He'd have to get Clay Latimer to the undertaker in Cactus Plain and then, as deputy sheriff in the booming town, and knowing the lawlessness that rampaged in the area every week, surely she would see his point of view?

Rod eased in the saddle again, a hombre of medium height, taut with muscle, clad in a grey flannel shirt and a flapping deerskin vest that had been made for him by old Red Cloud, a Mojave Indian who came periodically into town for white man's tobacco.

He had still another twenty miles to go through Cactus County, that area of land which cornered to the great Colorado River and Lake Havasu, where the desert gave way to grassland, mesquite and clumps of cottonwood and oaks. Here the big ranches lay, with the herds in the valleys where the water-holes were found.

Juana Ranch was one of the biggest and old man John Lopez was a pal of his, now highly concerned with big-time rustling and the rannies who got away with it. But this corner of Arizona was booming under the impact of railroad building and the scores of Irish labourers who hammered at the ties and spent their weekends drinking and gambling in either Cactus Plain or the outlaw town of Turtle Back. With gold being panned in the Little Creek that fed into the Colorado, and silver in the distant hills, there were many people on the move.

Not all were lawless; Cactus Plain had its little quota of church-going folk who sang weekly in the little adobe mission, and the ladies of the town patronised some neat little stores and held sewing classes. Preacher Thomas was a fine little man with a pene-trating eye and a fiery manner of delivering a sermon. Many a time he had wagged an admonishing finger at Rod Kane. The deputy shifted in the saddle again and smiled slightly as he mused.

The slow plodding of the tired animal took it over shale ridges and through boulder-strewn plains for about another six miles, to a point where the clumps of brown grasses became more frequent. He was reaching for his water bottle, knowing there was just about enough to see him and the horse safely to Cactus Plain, when the horse whinnied a sudden greeting.

Rod Kane patted the big black, saw its pricked-up ears, the distended nostrils.

He didn't actually reach for his Colt but his hand hung close to the well-worn holster.

He waited, cautiously, for one never knew the type of man who might be encountered in these badlands.

The hombre who suddenly jigged a grey stallion from behind the jagged heap of wind and sand-scoured boulders grinned cheerfully and held up a hand in greeting.

'Howdy! Now ain't that a dead man on that hoss?'

'It is,' Rod acknowledged. 'You can see that ...'

'Sure, sure – I'm jest talkin', mister. My name's Jim North – they call me Long Haired Jim.' The man laughed heartily.

'That figgers,' Rod smiled tiredly.

The other man wore the dirtiest collection of garments Rod had ever seen, and his black hair was longer than any Indian's. It fell to his shoulders in lank disarray, under a battered hat that had a bullet hole in it, and a dirty turkey feather set at an angle. His shirt was a faded red, torn and buttonless, and dirty with particles of old food and dust and sweat. He wore a weathered pair of leather trousers – the best thing about him – and a ragged broadcloth vest with torn pockets.

His bandana was a filthy shade of white and stained with blood that had long dried up.

There was one neat thing about him – his pearl-handled gun lay in a low cutaway holster and the gunbelt was a polished circle of brown leather that any man might envy.

'I'm a-heading for Cactus Plain,' said Long Haired Jim. 'Is that where you're takin' that cadaver?'

'It is,' agreed Rod Kane.

'Who is he?'

8

'A hellion named Clay Latimer. Well known in Cactus Plain.'

'Is that so? And you a deputy I can see by that badge! Waal, ain't often I have the law for company – me, I'm a bit of a wanderer …'

He jigged his grey stallion close to Rod's black, grinning disarmingly, and the odour of an unwashed body was pretty powerful. He glanced again at the led horse. 'I'm from way out. You don't mind if I tag along for a chaw of baccy and a chat?'

Rod looked him over again. 'I don't mind. I don't carry baccy and my mouth is dryer than a clay patch in August – I won't be talkin' much.' With that he urged the black on again, got some more motion out of the tired haunches. Long Haired Jim followed, slouching in the saddle, amused. He took out a twist of black tobacco and bit some off and generously offered some to Rod.

'No thanks, amigo. Not for me.' Rod glanced at the gunbelt. 'That's a mighty fine .45 you pack. But don't you find a pearl handle lacks some grip?'

'Nope – not this one! Too many notches in it.'

'Notches? You've killed with that gun?'

'I only killed one ranny – an' he was trying to steal my hoss – and that wasn't with this gun. The jasper I plugged had a pardner and he got clean away – except for one thing. He left this gun behind.'

Rod nodded. 'And now you tote it?'

'Waal, I carry it around. Mighty fine gun. I reckon some day I'll find the galoot who owned it …'

'Maybe if it's got all those notches, you'd better step clear of him.'

Long Haired Jim grinned again, the dirt on his sun-blackened face cracking a bit. 'Yup. Trouble is he took my pack-hoss – with four gunny sacks of gold. My gold!'

'That was tough.'

'It was, friend. Specially as he and his pardner didn't own to a hoss a-tween 'em but come creepin' up on me at night.'

'How'd he drop the gun?'

'Waal, jest afore he rode out of range I took some shots at him – after I'd killed his side-kick – an' one just nicked his wrist I reckon, and he dropped that pearl-handled forty-five.'

'So you got a swap for your gold and horses,' commented Rod Kane. 'One gun!'

'Yep. One gun – fer all that darned digging in the Little Horn mountains …'

'So that's where you came from?'

'I told you, friend, I'm from way out. Sure, I had a claim up in the Little Horn – worked it out.'

'And now you mosey around looking for the gent who drygulched you and took your gold?'

'That's it. Maybe I'll find him in Cactus Plain. I know one thing. I know the name of the galoot who toted this shooter …'

'How come?'

'Met this rider … see … an' we went together into Dry Sands, a little burg with a big gambling tent. I was playing cards when a man asks me about this gun – jest like you did. He'd seen the pearl butt and figured it kind of unusual. So he asked me about it an' I told him my story – jest the way I told you. and you know what he said?'

'You'd better tell me,' advised Rod Kane.

'This is the gun of Gideon James!'

The casual answer hit at Rod right through his tiredness and lack of real interest in the other's tribulations.

Gideon James was probably one of the most infamous outlaws and desperadoes of the West. The name was heard throughout Arizona, as far north as Utah, and down to Mexico. The fame of Gideon James had spread far and the stories of his deeds decorated many a bar conversation.

'Are you sure?' Rod asked slowly. 'What proof have you got?'

'This feller in Dry Sands had known Gideon James – but personally. He was all set to go fer his gun when I told him my tale, an' then he jest laughed and laughed. An ornery cuss, but I don't doubt he knew what he was talking about.'

Long Haired Jim hoisted the .45 out of the carefully oiled holster and showed it to Rod, butt first.

'See them? Twelve notches on this side an' four on the other. Kind of spoils the pearl-work – but sure gives a mighty fine grip. An' I reckon this feller Gideon James didn't bother to notch up Injuns and Mexicans …'

11

Rod nodded, again briefly. 'If you want my advice, Jim, you ought to forget about nosing around for this man. He'll have another gun by now. You wouldn't want to be just another notch on a new gun, huh?'

The other grinned. 'Oh, I ain't a-goin' to be another notch on any man's hogleg, Mister Deputy. I've been putting in a lot o' practice with this pearl-handled shooter – and I can tell you this gun has some magic.'

'Magic? That's crazy …'

'Crazy, is it? Waal, I don't think so. I figger some of the dead-shot magic has rubbed off on this gun. I can't go wrong with this hogleg, mister. It's fast – so fast it seems to leap into my hand like it was alive. It's quicker than a mountain cat. It never fails. I can clear leather faster with this gun than anything I ever owned in my life. It's uncanny! Now I tell you, when I meet up with Gideon James this here gun is sure going to be the end of him.'

'You're loco. Gideon James will outdraw you. You'll end up on Boothill.'

Long Haired Jim laughed uproariously.

'You watch this, Mister Deputy.' He paused. 'Did I git your name?'

'I'm Rod Kane.'

'Yep – watch this!' The saddle tramp holstered the gun, rubbed his hands for a few seconds, wiped them on his tattered vest and then drew the ornamental .45 with an astoundingly swift motion and fired as fast as the eye could blink at a nearby spindle-shaped cactus.

12

The slug nicked the cactus stem and the echo died away in the smell of gunsmoke.

Rod nodded. 'That's pretty fast, but a cactus ain't a man.'

'Waal, maybe I'll jest get Gideon James with a Winchester,' drawled the other, and he patted the rifle in the saddle-holster.

Rod nudged the black again. 'When I rode out of Cactus Plain there wasn't any talk of Gideon James bein' in town. We'd have known.'

He watched Long Haired Jim spit out a stream of baccy juice. Then: 'Could be I'm on the wrong trail. But maybe I'm not. Anyway, I'm a gent with plenty o' time. Reckon I'll not see my gold again but I aim to fill Gideon James full of holes with his own gun.'

2

Ready for Burial

When Rod Kane rode into the straggling town and Long Haired Jim went off with a casual wave, he prodded the black straight to the undertaker's office and climbed down wearily from his saddle and stiffly approached the led horse. Daylight was fading and he was bone tired and hungry. He wished to hell he could wallow in a bathtub but maybe he needed to eat and drink first. Even so, all this had to come after he had got rid of the body..

As he untied the dead man, he noted grimly that rigor mortis had set in. It was his distasteful task to carry the corpse inside the office. He had seen old man Herb Mason peering out of the window, and behind him the prim face of his wife, and as he hoisted the body to his shoulder the door of the clapboard building opened. Herb Mason allowed him to carry the dead man past his living room to the mortuary at the rear.

'Who is it?' snapped the little man. 'Goshdarn this dust. Mrs Mason won't like this.'

'Nobody likes nothing,' gritted Rod Kane. 'Least of all me! This cuss is Clay Latimer – as you'll see in a moment.' The deputy put the body down on the long plank used for this purpose.

'Latimer? Huh, that young hellion. Well, there's more like him.' Herb Mason smiled. 'Smells! Time he was buried. How long have you been on the trail?'

'Too damned long,' snapped Rod, anger stirring low in his guts. 'You take it, Mr Mason. I'll get the sheriff to come over and identify the body – an' maybe some other feller who knew him. Then you can bury him …'

The small undertaker rubbed his forehead. 'What did he do?'

'You should know,' said Rod brutally. 'You buried his victim. He shot a man in the back after an argument in the Last Chance saloon.'

'Aw – that. Been two deaths since then, Deputy. One nice and private – old Heinie the storekeeper dropped down dead yesterday. I buried him fast and gave the widow the bill a lot faster!' A thin grin crossed Herb Mason's withered face.

'I'm getting out of here,' muttered Rod. 'Right now I'm sick an' tired of guns an' death.'

He was so stiff from hours in the saddle that he staggered as he walked the two horses along to the livery that lay behind the brick and clapboard building that bore the legend: SHERIFF'S OFFICE.

16

He spent a few minutes with the Mexican wrangler. He slid his own saddle off the black, dumped it in a corner because he was too weary to do any more. He gave instructions that the horses were to be fed and watered and rubbed down. Kane wasn't greatly concerned about Clay Latimer's mount – the man wouldn't need it again – but the horseflesh was entitled to some consideration.

So it was some time later when he left the livery and set off to see Sheriff Joe Clark in his neat house on the west side of the town.

Rod Kane never reached the place.

He was passing the noisy saloon, The Imperial, one of the two drinking joints in Cactus Plain, when two men left the shadowy boardwalk just past the lighted windows. Something about their swift approach warned Rod of trouble, but he wasn't so sure. Instinctively, he halted, his hand near his gun butt. The oncoming men were striding quickly, without any hint of gunplay, and they were not drunk, although they seemed to have emerged from the saloon. They separated when only four yards from the deputy.

Rod noted their appearance in a fast glance of mental assessment that was part of his job.

'Kane!' sneered one of the men. He was tall, unshaven, young, with an insolent expression. His nose was thick and ugly, his mouth a thin slit which curled when he spoke. He wore clean clothes, a checked shirt and tight whipcord pants, a gunbelt that sagged to suit his long arms.

The other man was a lot older than his friend, thick-set and bearded. Even in the poor light of the street, with only yellow lamps gleaming from The Imperial, the nearest oil-burning street lamp twenty yards away, his deep-set eyes under thick brows seemed brutal and implacable.

'What the hell d'you want?' Rod stood his ground, an itch of mounting fear and dire foreboding crawling up his spine. He knew he should reach for his gun. But that would spark off Colt-play and maybe it would not come to that. Maybe they just wanted to be plenty mean about something. A deputy sheriff got plenty of this sort of treatment.

'Killer,' breathed the young man. 'You plugged Clay Latimer.'

'So that's it. You pals of his?'

'Sort of. We rode together Me an' Dirk here kinda liked ole Clay.'

'He killed a man – murder!' said Rod sharply.

'So you say. We know all about it. It was an accident.'

'Shot in the back?' Rod flicked wary glances right and left, moved back a bit.

'Jest an accident,' said the man called Dirk in his husky tones. 'Like my segundo, Bert, says – an accident.'

Timing their movements together, the two hefty men jumped at the deputy, arms swinging, their bodies presenting considerable momentum, enough to steamroll a man to the ground. Rod Kane was to be rough-housed; no gunplay, but he could be near to death by the time these two finished with him.

He didn't have much chance. He'd been in the saddle for days, without decent grub, suffering excessive heat and lack of sleep. He was wily enough to dodge the initial rush, just evading the clumsy, confident men, but having to face them again as they turned and stamped closer to him. More fists rammed out and one caught him an ugly thump down the side of his head. As Rod retaliated savagely with two fists, another blow landed, stunning his brain a bit. The red mist rolled – and cleared. He dodged another slamming arm by ducking and backing. He grabbed the fist of the old man – Dirk – and heaved the man forward. This threw the rangehand off balance, and Rod chopped a bunched fist down on the man's neck as he stumbled, almost bent double.

But Bert, the one with the bulbous nose, had just got into his stride and he rammed two blows at Rod that connected and staggered him backwards. Boots dug desperately into the dusty roadway. Rod felt blood trickle warmly down his lips as he regained balance and straightened, fists and arms raised like a barricade in anticipation of further hammering blows. They came as Bert waded into a tired man, arms swinging under the impetus of fresh muscles and a few tots of whisky. During this attack, the older man managed to heave Rod's arms around behind his back, shoved a knee into the small of his back, and held him, struggling.

'Get him!' snarled Dirk. 'Give him hell – the dang-blasted swine!'

Bert needed few instructions on how to take care of a well-nigh defenceless man. He slammed his fists into Rod's face in a rapid flurry. It was a vicious onslaught that took a man's face and body as a punch-bag.

Rod Kane slumped, as many a man might, his brains reeling towards the blackness that surged up to claim him. His arms were heavy chunks of lead that would not respond. His head took blow after blow. His vision clouded and his legs gave way. Only the fact that the man called Dirk held him up kept him from collapse.

They were all set to break his very frame when an interruption came from out of the gloom. Rod sprawled in the dirt, a booted foot ready to stamp down on his outstretched hand.

'I'll bust his hand! He'll never fire a Colt again ...'

'Hold it!' The barking, angry voice cut the night air. 'Unless you two jaspers want belly-slugs!' The jingle of spurs added to the interruption.

Bert whipped around, his feet coming together on the dirt just to give himself balance. All thought of smashing Rod Kane's gun-hand vanished as he stared into a sixgun held in a smartly-gloved hand.

Dirk, older and maybe a little wiser, inched away from the sprawling deputy, crouched and stared at the intruder. There was no sign around the man's neck saying he was a gunman; it was just there, unmistakable in the thin smile on the moustached face and the firm, confident way the big Frontier Colt was held. The hand lay in the brown glove as if it was a second skin; the finger itched on the trigger ready to unleash sudden death. The man's stance was that of a dancer, poised, cool and ready. His clothes were good; a silk shirt rippled over good chest muscles. His hat was a real Stetson and the best in the price range.

As Dirk's eyes dropped, he saw the shining black boots and knew they were the best of hand craftsmanship.

He got all this in seconds of sudden inward fear that hit his belly and helped him memorise fast.

'All right, stranger – we're going,' Dirk stammered.

'Who the heck are you?' rasped Bert, stupidly aggressive.

'Do you intend to back up?' murmured the man with the gun. 'Or would you like to try a draw? I can oblige by holstering this sixshooter. Just let me know.'

'This ain't your fight!' Bert wanted to argue.

'Git some sense!' snapped his partner. 'Let's go. Reckon we've given this deputy something to think about. Hell – are you comin', Bert?'

The man decided to agree. He turned, swaggered away, fingers hooked in his gunbelt. As he moved, he turned his head and spat at Rod Kane as he stirred uneasily on the road.

Rod Kane got up, a series of slow movements that hurt every muscle and sinew in his body, and he stood uncertainly in the gloom eyeing his rescuer. He saw the handsome, confident face, the clean silk shirt, the brown leather gunbelt and the now holstered gun. He got the same impression that Bert and Dirk had received – that this man was a professional gunman, a hard man of the frontier.

Rod muttered, 'Many thanks, stranger. You've done me a favour ...'

'Might have been better if I'd got on the scene a bit earlier. Those two bums seem to have roughed you up.'

'They had the advantage,' said Rod grimly. 'But next time they set on a lawman, they'll end up in the hoosegow.'

The thin moustached lips curved in a smile and the man turned and waved a casual farewell, his lithe body as graceful as a mountain cat in even these small motions.

'Say, who am I obliged to?' called out Rod Kane.

'The name is Smith,' drawled the man from the street gloom. 'Al Smith.'

'Rod Kane. Many thanks for your intervention, Al Smith ...'

'Think nothing of it,' came the cool response and the man sauntered away.

The deputy dusted his clothes and smiled slightly through split lips. He had no doubt that Al Smith had more than one name. He had noticed the casual way the man had enunciated the words, as if he didn't believe there was any significance in a name.

Rod wiped blood and dust from his face and swore. Hell, he was in a terrible state but he would have to see the sheriff just the same and give him the news about Clay Latimer. Then maybe a clean-up somewhere – probably in a tub in Sheriff Joe Clark's back room – and he'd be all set to go along and see June Latimer. He'd have to see her that night, in the little rooms behind her dress shop. The shop would be closed, but it wasn't too late to attempt some faltering explanations to the girl. He'd just have to do it!

When he rapped on the sheriff's door he waited a few moments for an answer. He looked around at the neat little garden area at the front of the small clapboard house and saw the hand of Muriel Clark, the sheriff's wife, in the layout of the clumps of red and blue flowers she so carefully tended. A matronly woman, she had made a cosy home for her husband and herself, a secure background for a man with an uncertain job and an unknown future.

Some moments later Rod Kane told his story to the sheriff. 'He's dead … at the undertaker's … he wanted to shoot it out …'

'Young hellion!' grunted Joe Clark. He tightened his belt, pulled in his paunch. His drooping grey moustache gave his round face a melancholy expression but this was deceptive. Sheriff Joe Clark was a matter-of-fact man with no illusions about his role in Cactus Plain. He had been handed a hard job because there were few applicants for the post, and only a genuine interest in law and elementary justice kept him at the task. He ran his hand through his scant greying hair. 'Waal, it had to come! He was a cocky

23

damned fool – been in every trouble you can name.'

'I want to see June Latimer as soon as possible,' said Rod, 'but I'd like to get rid of this blood and trail dust first. Can I use that big wood tub of yours, Joe?'

Muriel Clark intervened. 'You certainly can, my boy. I'll get some hot water – good thing we've got a big kettle nearly boiling on the stove. Oh dear, you men! Can you not find yourselves some nice easy work, like Mr Anson at the hardware store, or a quiet little spread somewhere?'

'Maybe you've got a point, Mrs Clark,' said Rod quietly. 'But we're doin' a job that someone – some-where – has to do.'

'Dear me, I've heard it all before,' sighed the lady, and she moved to the big, round iron stove in the centre of the room.

'Those two rats who jumped you,' began the sheriff. 'Dirk and Bert, you say? Any other names?'

'I never heard any … too busy tryin' to stay on my feet.'

'I'll find them,' growled the sheriff. 'I'll run 'em out of town. Pals of Clay Latimer, huh? I'll nose around in the morning.'

'Might do that myself. I don't take kindly to being made a punch-bag. One thing – I was sure glad this Al Smith character showed up. Know anything about him?' Rod described the man so far as he could remember. 'A smooth feller – a gunny, I think …'

'Hmm, we've got a select circle like that in town,' muttered Joe Clark, 'and this one doesn't rightly stand

24

out in my mind. I don't know every galoot in Cactus Plain – and strangers arrive every day. Still, gunmen are a kind that's easy to identify...'

Rod got into the hot tub a bit later and, with the door closed and a chunk of soap in one hand and a scrubber in the other, he swiftly got rid of dust and sweat. When he climbed out of the steaming water, he felt a lot better – but hungry. Some of the aches and pains had vanished. But he was not so concerned about that; he urgently wanted to get around to see June Latimer, to personally explain the grim situation that had led to the death of her brother.

He dressed swiftly, having to make do with his trail-stained clothes, although he beat the dust out of his brown pants and flannel shirt. When he walked into the living room of the sheriff's house, Muriel Clark forced some food on him.

'You've got to eat. I can guess what you've been eating for days – jerky beef and coffee.'

Finally he stepped out into the dark street. He patted his gun holster and pulled his hat down, instinctive movements of a man setting himself for an unpleasant task. He walked down the main stem, pass-ing a parked buckboard, and wondered just exactly how he would start his explanations to the girl. Of course, she knew by now that he had ridden out after Clay after the shooting in the Last Chance, but she probably thought that Clay would elude his pursuer. The young fellow had been in plenty of trouble before and hearing about his escapades was nothing new to

June Latimer. He'd ridden out of town in a hurry a number of times and he inevitably turned up again to drink and gamble and cheat any gullible stranger in town. It was suspected he had robbed old man Green field's store but that little episode some six months ago had been hard to pin on him. Clay's pals had given him an alibi.

Rod Kane slowed when he approached the now-darkened little dress shop owned by June Latimer. He knocked on the heavy wooden door, took off his hat and waited.

When the door opened a shaft of yellow light from a lamp illuminated the passage and living room beyond. The girl stared into Rod's troubled face.

'You! Why? Why?' She was nearly crying, choking out the useless words. Her dark hair fell in long waves down her neck. Even in the uncertain light, he saw the grief in her dark eyes. Her hands made gestures to him as if trying to push him away.

'You know?' he said huskily. 'Someone has told you – already! June – I was forced into the gun-fight—'

'You – you didn't have to ride after him—'

'It was my job. The sheriff was busy elsewhere. Clay had killed a man …'

'You – of all people – you killed my brother!' she burst out.

'I tried to get here as fast as possible, to explain, June,' he muttered, and then he stared along the lighted passage. A man emerged from the living room.

It was the tall figure of Al Smith.

3

Working for Nothing

Long Haired Jim North elbowed down to the bar counter and sniffed appreciatively at the thick tang of ale and whisky that hung in the air. He spat his well-chewed baccy plug out of his mouth, aiming at the sawdust at his feet, and then he raised the mug of ale to his lips and drank noisily.

Without any doubt he needed the drink. It washed away all the memories of hours and days on the trail; the times when the sun had beat at him and mocked him for his futile search for Gideon James and his vanished gold.

Yet Long Haired Jim knew he wouldn't have it any other way. He was a born wanderer. He'd stopped riding the ridges and valleys when he had found the gold in the Little Horn mountains; he had stopped wandering only long enough to file a claim, and all had been for nothing.

'Nuthin'!' he muttered aloud. 'Nuthin'! All that gold – jest gone! Me – working myself to the bone and jest to make that ornery gun-slick Gideon James rich!'

'You say something, pardner?' The man standing next to Long Haired Jim turned slightly and surveyed the wanderer with deep-set eyes. His husky voice made the inquiry again. 'You say somethin'?'

'Jest talkin' to myself.'

'Yeah? Well, that's a loco habit. Still you look like you've been on rough trails for a long time.'

'I sure have. I bin around by Signal Butte, up in the hills near the Mojave Reservation, follered the Colorado for some ways, looked in at Danby and Live Oaks ...'

'Just trail happy?' sneered the man with the deep-set eyes.

'Nope. I'm lookin' for a certain galoot.'

'Waal, this town is full of drifters.' The man spoke contemptuously, taking in Long Haired Jim's dirty appearance. 'What's your name, feller?'

'Jim North. Folks call me Long Haired Jim.'

'You look like a blamed Injun,' said the other. 'And you stink like a polecat.'

The wanderer eyed the bearded face casually and as he picked up his ale again he said, 'What's your name, amigo?'

'Dirk – Dirk Jordan – if that's any interest to a saddlebum.'

'Don't interest me none. I'm lookin' for a man called Gideon James ...'

Dirk Jordan had gone into the saloon to fortify himself after the encounter with Rod Kane. He had left Bert Skinner talking to a saloon girl in a corner of the smoke-filled place. He had brooded over the fight, examined his bruised knuckles, and was sufficiently satisfied about the punishment he and Bert had handed out to the killer of old Clay Latimer. Clay had been a good friend, the sort of young hellion who was handy in any lawless exploit, and they had carried off some neat little hold-ups in the past. Too bad he was dead, plugged by that mangey deputy.

Dirk turned again to the saddle tramp. His brutal, deep-set eyes allowed some amusement. 'Say, I've heard of Gideon James. He's an outlaw. Why in the name o' hell should you look for him?'

'I jest want to kill him,' said Long Haired Jim.

'You're loco!' Laughter belched from Dirk's lips.

'Maybe you've seen Gideon James?' inquired Long Haired Jim.

'Me? Wouldn't know him from General Grant. Just heard the name – that's all.'

'I was told he might be in Cactus Plain.'

'A galoot like that don't advertise his presence,' sneered Dirk. 'Most likely he'll be some place under another name.'

'Yep, so I figgered.'

'You're loco – an' you stink. Get the hell away from me. Why the blazes am I talkin' to a bum like you? Beat it, before I poke a fist into that dirty pan you call a face.' Dirk Jordan had tired of the encounter.

'My money is as good as yours – and I aim to drink my ale right here,' said Long Haired Jim.

He reached out for his mug again, with the intention of draining it and buying a replacement, and the next moment a big arm chopped down on his wrist. The mug of beer jerked and tilted on its side.

'I've told you – you got a smell worse'n a nest of polecats. I reckon you ought to jump in a horse-trough.'

The fat bartender in a white apron stared from the other side of the pine counter. Long Haired Jim caught his eye. 'Say, friend, fill my mug with ale. I reckon to drink my fill.'

The next moment thick heavy arms descended on the wanderer's thin frame and he was propelled a few yards away from the counter. Jim North's dirty red shirt was torn a bit more as, with a surprisingly wiry spring, he shook free from Dirk Jordan's grip and faced the man.

'I aim to drink here,' repeated the long haired man.

Dirk backed to the counter again, his thin mouth slitted in amusement. The red of his lips showed like a line against his black beard.

'Git! You smell! Hell, you look like a dirty Injun. You're annoyin' decent men who want to drink in comfort.'

Dirk Jordan was sure his bullying would have the desired effect. The thin black-haired drifter would, of course, just slink away. These bums were gutless …

All at once the pearl-handled gun literally sprang into the black-haired man's hand and pointed, steady and ominous, at Dirk Jordan's belly.

'You've got things wrong,' murmured Long Haired Jim. 'You can back away from that bar an' let an honest man drink.'

'Why you skinny rat! Put that gun away. You wouldn't kill a man just to git a drink! You can't buffalo me!'

The fancy .45 was holstered immediately. Among the crowd of men who had backed away to give the two fair space, more than a few noticed the speed with which the gun was handled. Even Dirk Jordan, for all his fondness for bullying, was suddenly wary and displeased with the way things were turning out.

'You can go for that hogleg you carry – any time,' said Long Haired Jim. 'And I'll oblige the undertaker with another cadaver!'

The pearl-butted gun lay like a small cannon in the holster. Men noted the weapon and some grinned, for Dirk Jordan and his sidekick, Bert Skinner, were not too well liked by the regular customers of the Last Chance.

Dirk felt the hard ridge of the pine counter pressing into his back, saw the grinning faces around him. Some of the cowboys and railroad workers were cautious, backing from the bar. Others looked up warily from their tables. Two saloon girls eased behind men for possible shelter. In a corner, Bert Skinner wiped his bulbous nose and stared and wondered what in tarnation Dirk had gotten into.

'You figger to go for your gun or are you all mouth?' sneered Long Haired Jim.

'Damn and blast you!'

Dirk's hand whipped for his gun butt. He had decided that this dirty saddle-tramp was bluffing and that the swift way he had handled the .45 was mere trickery, probably an illusion.

Red rage urged him on. He tugged at his gun and then froze in utter disbelief, his hand clammy and tingling, the gun only half-way out of leather.

He stared once more at the pearl-handled Colt, at the black barrel pointed right at his chest. The gun had leapt into position, it seemed. Few men could draw so fast and those who could were legendary and never dirty drifters with 'aimlessness' written all over them.

The notched, pearl-handled gun did not roar. It merely pointed grimly at the man. Dirk's weapon dropped back into leather and his hand came slowly away.

'Now beat it – unless you want to try again,' breathed Long Haired Jim. 'Beat it, move out an' let me have my ale! Get goin'!'

Wordless snarls throbbed from Dirk Jordan's lips and he glanced wildly to right and left for support. He saw only smiles and blank looks. Even Bert Skinner hung back in the far corner of the room. Some men, at a table, intent on pursuing their card game, gave some displeased advice. 'Git goin'! You heard what the bum said! Git. You're upsetting our game.'

Dirk had survived in lawless towns because he knew when to retreat. This was one of those times. With his gun lying heavily in its holster, he lumbered towards the doors, conscious that the pointed pearl-butted Colt followed his trek in an unrelenting arc. He reached the batwings and pushed through; then paused outside, clenching his fists in a rage. He had half a mind to stamp back into the saloon and see if he could get the edge on the trail-stained drifter. Then he remembered the speed of that draw and years of experience urged caution.

'I'll git that no-account – somehow!' he muttered and strode away.

As Long Haired Jim drank deeply of a new glass of ale, and the men at the bar returned to their arguments, an old man with a head as bald as an egg and as toothless as a new-born babe came up to him.

'Hey, that's a mighty fine gun, mister. Pearl, huh? Now I knowed a galoot who packed a Colt like that …'

The other man turned a dirty, sun-blackened face. He said cautiously, 'Yeah? Who?'

'Was a smooth jasper,' yapped the oldster. 'Right over in Texas a year ago, near El Paso. I was shotgun guard on a stage …'

'You?' grinned Long Haired Jim.

'Shore! I ain't as old as I look. Jest because I ain't got no teeth—'

'Who was the ranny who packed a gun like this?' interrupted Long Haired Jim.

'Why, it was Gideon James! Everybody knows he

33

carried a pearl-handled .45 – an' it had twelve notches one side an' four on t'other ...' His voice broke off as Jim North silently drew the gun from leather and displayed the butt.

'Take a good look, old-timer.'

'Them notches! Why, this is the gun of Gideon James!'

'Yeah. Don't get excited. It won't bite.'

'How come you tote the gun around?' spluttered the little baldy man.

'It's a long story and I ain't in the mood.'

Pale little eyes searched Long Haired Jim's sun-cracked face. The oldster began to back away as a sudden fear seemed to hit him, and he was only detained by Jim's hand.

'Seein' you got such big ears for a little man an' know so much, maybe you know where Gideon James is hiding out these days?'

'I – I – don't want to tangle with this,' yapped the oldster.

'You were mighty keen to air your views a moment ago. What are you worryin' about?'

'Don't you know?' breathed the old man.

'I know nuthin' till you tell me.'

The old man looked around to reassure himself and then on an impulse he hissed: 'Gideon James is in Cactus Plain, but not many knows that! An' if I were you, pardner, I'd throw that gun away an' ride out of town!'

*

When Rod Kane saw the tall lithe figure emerge from June Latimer's back living room and stand smiling in the passage, surprise halted his words and movements. He stared at the suave smiling man while June threw out more bitter denunciations.

'I'll hate you, Rod Kane, as long as you live! For you, of all men, to shoot down Clay!' She choked. 'He wasn't bad – he was just easily led. No one tried to help him …'

'That's not true, June.' Rod found grating words. 'The sheriff handed out fatherly advice long ago, but it was thrown back in his face.'

'Did you have to shoot to kill?'

'He was all-fired set to kill me!' Rod ground out.

She raised her fists, hammered at his chest. 'I hate you – hate you! Go away!'

'I just wanted to tell you what happened. But I see someone else got here first.' Rod flung a bitter glance at Al Smith. 'So you moseyed along here as soon as you heard the news? What made you come here?'

'We re old friends …' began Al Smith smoothly.

'Old friends? You weren't even in town when I rode out.'

'I made Miss Latimer's acquaintance the first hour I was in Cactus Plain,' said the other quietly. 'We are now good friends. In a few days, Kane, a relationship can develop.'

'Who the devil are you?'

'What do you mean by that?'

'Where have you come from?'

35

'You name it, I've been there,' said Al Smith softly.

'That's not an answer. You could be anybody. Smith isn't your name.'

'Maybe.'

'I can make inquiries,' said Rod Kane grimly. 'The town marshal at Parkerville is a good friend.'

'Are you trying to accuse my friend of something?' blazed the girl. 'As you are so curious, I can tell you that Mr Smith is a gentleman from Texas – from Cimarron, if you must know. He has a cattle ranch out there.'

Rod nodded. 'All right – all right. So he's here on business. Everybody in Cactus Plain is here on business – even the rogues.'

Al Smith took easy strides to the deputy, his gun swinging easily in the polished holster. As he approached, Rod saw for the first time the colour of the man's hair, now that he was hatless. He had good wavy hair, blond and well cared-for. He was admittedly good-looking, the kind the ladies would favour.

'Watch your tongue, Deputy,' the man advised.

'I am doin' just that,' retorted Rod. 'So you have cattle interests out Texas way?'

'That's true – if it's any of your business.'

'June Latimer is my friend – that makes it my business.'

The other smiled. 'I believe she mentioned you once during our many delightful conversations.'

'And you just had to dash along here to tell her I'd reached town with her brother's dead body?'

'I'm afraid you got it wrong, Kane.'

'You fool, Rod!' flashed the girl. 'I heard about you from Mrs Mason! She came tearing along to tell me you'd brought Clay to their mortuary. Then, minutes later, Mr Smith called.'

Rod fought to get a grip on the situation. He was still terribly tired and the aches were returning to his body. He said hotly making the whole thing worse, 'So you entertain a strange man at night in your rooms!'

'I – I – didn't ask Mr Smith to call at this hour,' faltered the girl.

'I'm to blame,' said Al Smith. 'I'm afraid I'm too impulsive. And I think this whole encounter has got out of hand. I suggest we leave, Kane, and talk things over when our tempers have cooled.'

It was good advice and Rod nodded, stepping back into the cool night air, a dismal feeling in the pit of his stomach. He had wanted to say such important things to the girl. He had wanted to tell her he loved her, even though it was an impossible situation for her to consider the man who had killed her brother. She hated him.

Al Smith had contributed to this lousy set-up, he was just the sort of man to offer consolation at a time when it was wanted. Rod cursed him, although the man had rescued him from permanent injury at the hands of the two hellions.

As Rod stood outside the dress shop window, the shutters folded over the small panes of glass, he was joined by the stranger, Al Smith.

'You know something, Kane,' said the tall man. 'You are making a big mistake in being so suspicious of me. I'll give you a tip, get in touch by telegraph to the Town Marshal at Cimarron, Texas, and ask about me. That's all.'

And with his expensive stetson tilted on his blond hair, the man walked away down the dusty main stem. The sound of his whistling carried through the night air, an old Reb tune that had been popular many years ago.

Rod expelled his breath, swearing at length to no one in particular, unless the green eyes of a black alley cat could be termed an audience. He was utterly fed up. His aches were returning – or was he just now conscious of them? Worse, he was sick at heart.

Rod swung around savagely and headed for the building with the weathered board: Sheriff's Office. He let himself into the dark building with the key he possessed, and then lit a lamp. As yellow light spilled out over the old desk, the rack of rifles, the three empty cells at the back of the big room, he tugged off his boots and unbuckled his gunbelt.

He sat on the big couch which had stood for years against the wall and wondered why he continued with this job. He supposed he had gotten fond of old Joe Clark and hated to even think of letting him down. No, he couldn't walk out on the job. Maybe if the sheriff stepped down and retired, he could think of quitting the business of lawman without compunction because it was a hard, unhappy task.

Rod allowed the rambling thoughts to filter through his tired head while he looked in a locker for a clean shirt. He kept a lot of gear in the office, using the place as a sort of home. Most other times he bunked in Joe Clark's house, in a spare room. Joe and Muriel had always made him welcome but he didn't like to intrude on their domestic life too much, so pretty often he bunked in the sheriff's office.

He cleaned his boots and polished them. He beat out the grit from his hat. He wiped his gunbelt and put it on again. Then he figured he'd go out and get a bite to eat because his guts were definitely rumbling. Then he'd return and probably drop dead asleep on the couch and to hell with everything until sunup.

About thirty-five minutes later he was coming out of the Chinese steak-house, having filled his stomach with good hot food and coffee, and was about to head for the sheriff's office, when he practically bumped into Long Haired Jim North.

They stopped under the glow of light from a lighted window in the side of The Imperial. Rod smiled.

'Hey, you still moseying around?'

'Yep. And I'm on to somethin'!'

'What in thunder do you mean by that?'

'I've jest got to know Gideon James is in Cactus Plain. Yessir, I'm a-goin' to meet up with that thieving dry-gulcher pretty soon.'

'I think you've had a skin-full.'

Long Haired Jim waved a hand calmly. 'Not drunk – not yet, pardner. Not too drunk to fill that outlaw full o' holes with his own hogleg – an' that's what I aim to do!'

'Yeah, you've told me all this before,' said Rod Kane. He paused. 'But you didn't tell me what Gideon James looked like. How'll you recognise him? The way I get your story, you jest got a fleeting glance of him as he rode away with your two hosses – and your gold.'

'Hah! I'm pretty smart!' Jim North wagged a dirty finger at the deputy. 'I ain't no fool. I'll show you somethin'. Reckon you ought to know about this, seeing you're a lawman.'

Long Haired Jim fished in a buttoned pocket on the left-hand side of his stained shirt. He pulled out a small printed handbill.

'There! That's him – wanted for murder – one Gideon James. I got the bill in Danby, from the sheriff there. Mighty fine feller, that sheriff. I told him I was goin' bounty huntin'. Now you read that, Mister Deputy, and you'll see how I know I'll recognise Gideon James. You should have one of these in your office, anyways.'

'Reckon we should,' admitted Rod Kane.

He read the description: 'Round-faced, dark pointed beard and moustache, thick dark hair and blue eyes and good teeth. Height: five feet eleven inches. Weight: one hundred and ninety pounds. No scars. Speaks with a Southern accent and is gentle-manly in manner …' Rod looked up and handed the worn bill back to the other man.

'Could fit a lot of hombres, ridin' the night trail,' he commented.

Long Haired Jim shook his head. 'Nope, Deputy. I just know I'll recognise that skunk when I sees him. I got a feelin' right here.' He placed a hand over his heart.

Rod's lean face creased in a grin again and he began to walk slowly. He got back to the office, locked the door and pulled off his boots. His gunbelt draped a nearby hatstand. Suddenly he realised how terribly weary his whole body had become, and he sank down to the couch.

He fell into a deep black sleep, and then, after a few hours, he began to swirl through crazy mixed up dreams.

He saw Al Smith's smooth face smiling so courteously, then it changed and became bearded and cruel and dark. Then, suddenly, it was the killer face of the outlaw Gideon James.

4

Wanted Handbill

When sunup came and warmth flooded the sheriff's office, Rod Kane woke up and, after some reflection, laughed away his crazy dream of the night. He had been tired, overwrought. He walked to a mirror, stared at the bruises on his face, the nasty crack in his lower lip. Just to grin was painful. He cursed the two hellions who had set on him and, with an ordinary man's human anger, wished he could hand out the same punishment to the two one-time pals of Clay Latimer. Maybe he would, at that.

He was musing about events when the sheriff opened the door and strode in. He glanced at Rod. 'Figured you'd be here. Why in heck didn't you stay at our house? Muriel was expectin' you.'

'You don't want a boarder,' Rod smiled. He changed the subject. 'Have we any Wanted handbills concerning Gideon James?'

43

'Gideon James? Maybe. What put that into your mind?'

'Just that drifter I met – Long Haired Jim he calls himself – says that Gideon James is in Cactus Plain.'

'If you listen long enough, you hear everythin',' growled Joe Clark. 'If Gideon James was in this town, I'd know. I've got two miserable ginks who make it their business to learn all sorts of information, and for a dollar they'd give away their own mothers. He ain't in this town, Rod.'

'You ought to know, Joe. All the same I'd like a look at the handbills.'

The sheriff had the key to the drawers in the big desk and without comment he leafed through some old Wanted posters and handed two over to the Deputy. Rod glanced at them. One was identical to the description Jim North toted around; the other was more interesting because it bore a crude drawing of the wanted outlaw. He studied the portrait, noting the thick dark beard and moustache, the dark wavy hair. a list of crimes giving dates and places was appended, which showed that Gideon James had travelled far and wide, a man of the trails and valleys, from Texas to Arizona, a loner mostly, except on odd occasions when he took a partner.

He apparently had had little to do with the gangs and groups of killers that hung around the frontier towns, seeming to prefer the owlhoot trails.

'This picture could fit a lot of men,' Rod commented.

'Maybe he's disappeared, hung up his guns, leading

44

a law-abiding life,' said the sheriff. 'Some of 'em do. Some change their names and git married an' settle down. One or two have become lawmen, strangely enough. I reckon anything can happen in this gosh-darned country ...'

'I'll tell that to Long Haired Jim next time I see him.'

Sheriff Joe Clark changed the subject. 'John Lopez rode into town yesterday, a few hours before you got back. He's plenty annoyed about the rustling that's going on around the Juana Ranch and he's threatening to order his hands to shoot on sight any rustler they catch.'

'Taking the law into his own hands?'

'It's not the first time a big ranch owner has set himself up as the law on his land.'

'John has a great respect for the due processes of law. He backed the appointment of Judge Anders.'

'Yep – reckon he's getting impatient. He told me he's lost a whole herd of steers since the last tally and his men have trailed the sign right up to Turtle Back.'

'Outlaw town itself! Well, it figures. Anything else?'

'Yeah. He wanted me to ride out to Turtle Back an' raise hell. I told him a dead sheriff was no good to anybody. I'm goin' out to the Juana Ranch soon as I git a bit of paper-work done.'

Smiling, Rod Kane stepped out, and walked along the main stem.

At the timber yard there were many a hoarse yell from the drivers. A man was taking down the shutters from a store, and two oldish men were painting the false-front of a hotel. The sun was beginning to climb, promising another warm day and no hint of rain for the sodbusters down the valley. In an alley, Mexican children and two dogs played in the dust, adding their yells to the almost musical ringing sounds of metal on metal that came from the blacksmith's shop.

Rod walked briskly and, inevitably, began to think of June Latimer. Her angry face – those dark eyes blazing at him – were stamped on his memory.

Momentarily lost in thought, and not so observant, he failed to notice the old Indian who stalked slowly behind him, solemnly keeping in exact stride, now that Rod had slowed his pace. The old Mojave was dressed in well-worn buckskins, his black hair parted and plaited and coyote tails hung from his waist. He carried an old trade musket cradled in his arms, a flintlock probably more than thirty years old.

A grin from a passer-by warned Rod and he wheeled quickly and laughed when he saw the Indian.

'Hey, Red Cloud, what are you doin' in town, as if I didn't know!'

Not a facial twitch cracked the expressionless face. 'Long time no see deputy … maybe you got baccy?'

'Don't see the stuff, Red Cloud, and darn well you know it. But let's go to the store and I'll buy you a twist.'

It was an old routine. Red Cloud would trail him with a morose expression, just walking paces behind, silent. Rod always knew what he wanted. It was a little game, played to an exact drill and ending with Red Cloud receiving his long twist of white man's tobacco. Rod didn't mind. Sometimes Red Cloud would part with some odd bit of information, garnered in the hills of the reservation – or Turtle Back, a place where he was tolerated on the supposition that he was of no account.

'All right – you got your baccy!' Rod smiled as they stood outside the store. 'Anythin' new, Red Cloud?'

The Indian just stared. For some time he hardly blinked. Rod waited for the grunting reply.

'White men … in Shadow Mountains …'

The words were punctuated with a thick accusing finger. Red Cloud stared once more, his black eyes unblinking. Thirty years ago he had been a warrior, a menace to wagon trains and pioneers, along with his brothers. But that was long past and now he wandered like a lonely figure.

'Shadow Mountains border the Indian Reservation,' remarked the deputy. 'White men shouldn't be there. Maybe they're not sure of their whereabouts, Red Cloud – it can happen. Anyway, what are they doing there?' He had to repeat the question.

'White men – dig.'

'Well, what are they digging for? D'you know, Red Cloud?'

He waited patiently again for the grunting reply.

'Dig for – lost mine! Make – big bang.'

Rod laughed. 'Oh, that again! The lost treasure!' La Mina Del Padre. Men had been after that cache for

47

over a hundred years. There was a mission near the Colorado River in that area and the padres got to know the Indians were about to attack. They gathered silver, gold and jewels from the mission – it seemed they had plenty – and hid it in an old mine shaft in the Shadow Mountain. Most of them were killed by the Indians later. Only one man survived to tell the tale – and his memory was faulty. The old shaft was never located again.

'Using dynamite,' commented Kane. 'Waal, the Shadow Mountains are a long way off – nigh on forty miles – but those men have no right up there. There's a State Order prohibiting white men from entering the Reservation.'

Red Cloud walked away, gripping his twist of tobacco.

Rod Kane strode on, feeling that he had made a dubious trade. It was not his duty to embark on a long trip into the Shadow Mountains unless the sheriff's office got definite orders from the County Office. The treasure seekers would sicken in time and move off, as many had done before them when they realised their venture was doomed to failure. For more years than the oldest man could count, there had been seekers after the treasure, and still the old shaft had remained unlocated. The story ran that the shaft had been filled in after the treasure had been cached, and then the survivor's mind had broken and he had been unable to recall the position of the shaft – except that it was in a certain part of the mountain. When, finally, searchers got around to looking for sign of an old mine shaft, wind and rain had eroded any indications of its position. And as the years went past, this, of course, got worse.

So now it was a legend, something that periodically men got the urge to search for.

'I figure that information was cooked up by Red Cloud jest to get himself a bit o' baccy,' mused Rod Kane, 'or maybe those galoots have been up there for some time ...'

He forgot the whole thing an hour later, when the morning sun glared down at Cactus Plain and, particularly, the cemetery on the inevitable hill. The burial of Clay Latimer was to take place that morning.

Rod was told about the funeral by a passer-by and he walked slowly to the site.

He saw June all in black, weeping and staring down at the gash in the yellow earth, and by her side was Al Smith, looking immaculate in a sombre black coat and trousers. He was wearing a gun, Rod Kane noticed at once, in his usual holster supported by his gunbelt. This man did not go far without his gun, it seemed, no matter what the occasion.

Rod was silent as the service proceeded and then when people started to move away he approached the girl.

'June – I'm sorry. What can I say? I sure never wished this ...'

'Then you should not have hunted Clay down.'

'Maybe you're right,' he said bitterly. 'Maybe I

should have handed in my badge long ago, when I first met you and realised you had a wild brother.'

'He wasn't bad!' she flashed. 'He just had terrible friends!'

He nodded. Of course, it was useless to argue now with her that Clay Latimer had been no-good for a long time and that he sought out his particular pals.

Rod Kane flicked at the man with grim eyes, prepared to accept the undoubted fact that June Latimer could choose her own friends – and in that second he saw the bland amusement in Al Smith's nonchalant gaze. Then the man's expression changed as he glanced down at the girl with deep concern, one hand on her arm as he guided her across the rough ground.

Rod knew at once that this man was more devious than honest. What was his game? Was he just attempting to gain the girl's affections? There could be nothing else, for June Latimer had little money and no position.

Rod Kane came away from Boothill determined to send the very telegram to Cimarron that Al Smith had so coolly suggested. Sure, it seemed crazy to make the inquiry. Why would he lie, give such obvious pointers to his identity if, in fact, everything wasn't true?

Well, maybe the man was bluffing. The world was full of characters who lied as if under a compulsion to do so.

On the other hand, it was so easily checked that only a fool would leave himself wide open to challenge

– and Al Smith was no fool.

Rod Kane often displayed a streak of obstinacy, and right now he was in that mood.

He went along to the telegraph office and got the operator to send the message to the Town Marshal at Cimarron, Texas.

'Please check identity of one Al Smith, purporting to be a rancher in Cimarron. Description: tall, blond, dark moustache, athletic build, well-dressed. Carries a .45 Frontier Colt. Oblige, R. Kane, Deputy Sheriff, Cactus Plain, Cactus County.'

Rod walked out grimly. There were times when a lawman's tasks were not so pleasant. He wondered if his dislike of Al Smith was based merely on jealousy. Once again, he thought: 'There's something. Damned if I can explain, but that galoot irks me. Maybe it's that durned gun. Figure he goes to bed with it.'

5

Gentleman Rancher

Sheriff Joe Clark rode his brown gelding at a steady trot for about four miles and then settled down to a good striding journey for another hour. He sat hard in the saddle and rolled a cigarette from his pouch of Bull Durham. The sun hit the back of his neck and possibly deepened the red-black tan another degree. Lighting the smoke with a yellow sulphur match, he considered the man, John Lopez.

Well, he was a gentleman, which was more than could be said for some ranchers. He came from good Spanish stock, although his mother had been Irish, hence his Christian name. He was rich and the ranch house at Juana Ranch was a reflection of his family wealth, a huge handsome place with a wide patio and a white adobe wall all around the courtyard. He employed both Mexican and white cowboys and made no discrimination. The Juana Ranch, with the brand of the Double J, ran in all four directions as far as a man could see from the Spanish-styled tower at the back of the ranch house. It was a land of gentle hills and valleys, generous with bunch grass, now browning under the summer heat.

John was justifiably incensed about the amount of rustling that was directed at his stock. The trouble seemed to be that the Juana Ranch stretched due south and one boundary ran roughly parallel with the trail leading to the outlaw town of Turtle Back. This black-spot, a collection of ramshackle shacks and gambling tents that had grown up around two large caves, used for years as hideouts for men on the run, had attracted many hardcases. Most of the inhabitants of Turtle Back dared not show face in any town. As for the others, they were drifters, or men who fancied a spell of hard gambling and drinking, probably with ill-gotten gains.

Joe Clark blew smoke out, sighed and urged on his horse. He'd have to make the crittur work.

He would have to advise John Lopez not to string up any rustler his men caught. He would tell the rancher that his men could not shoot to kill the moment they spotted a strange rider on the land. Innocent men could die that way. He had emphasised this point the other day but John was in such an angry mood that he had hardly listened. Maybe he'd find him in a calmer frame of mind this time. He hoped so, because by the time he got back to Cactus Plain the day would be all shot and it was a long ride if there was no result.

54

The trail wound around the base of small hills and bore the imprint of many hoof-marks made when the ground had been wet. It was mostly cowboys who passed this way. The railroad men were on the other side of Cactus Plain, getting nearer every week with their iron road.

Sheriff Joe Clark squinted at the sun, estimating the time with shrewdness – although he wore a gold Albert watch – and pulled his black hat down a bit more. If the gelding kept up this pace, he'd be in sight of the Juana Ranch buildings in little over another hour.

Miles beyond the ranch, near Turtle Back, the desert encroached on the fertile lands, with weird Joshua trees and cholla cactus filling the ravines. Here the land was covered with spring flowers, lavender crocus. Here and there he saw the shining wax-like whiteness of the first yucca blooms and the small new mesquite leaves shooting up. And if a man lifted his head and stared at the immensely distant horizon, he could just make out the blue tinge of the Little Horn mountains.

Musing, lulled by the even motion of his horse, Joe Clark did not notice the three riders half-hidden by the clump of old oaks that made a glade on the hill-side.

But the sheriff's approach had been observed for some minutes by the group and one had even used a spy-glass to ascertain the identity of the lone rider.

He was a huge man, fat and ugly, wearing a grey top

hat and a dirty frock coat. His red shirt was tight over his chest and belly and contrasted absurdly with the hat, which had seen better days.

Lowering the spy-glass he said, 'Fate is a strange old hag, my friends! Consider! Here we have the sheriff of Cactus Plain riding so innocently in our direction.' His rich, fruity voice hinted at a wasted education.

His two companions were lean, unshaven, cold-eyed and as alike as two peas in a pod. Wind and sun and long hours in a saddle had fashioned them.

'That blamed badge-toter!' The man spat out the words.

'Told me to git out o' town!' hissed the other. 'And I got – because he was prodding me with a six-gun.'

'I have no liking for the gentleman myself,' observed the big man. 'He had the effrontery to accuse me of murder and theft and thrust a Wanted handbill before my eyes when I was in the act of drinking whisky with a friend. There was little I could do except produce a gun and back out of the saloon – a noisy place, in truth, with some rather low company.'

'Yeah – we know all about it.'

'A damned handbill with my good name – Sam Hadfield – in big, unseemly letters!' exclaimed the fat man indignantly. 'What do you think of that, Mick?'

'Durned insult,' grinned the lean man.

'And you, Nat?'

The man spat. 'D'you aim to let this coyote pass – or d'you figger to rough him up?'

'I think we could teach him a lesson of sorts without

56

any real trouble to ourselves. And why not? The law is no friend to us.'

Sheriff Joe Clark heard the hoarse laughter and the rapid thud of on-coming hooves almost simultaneously. He whipped a look at the three surging riders and rowelled his horse at once. The animal squealed in protest but flung at once into a headlong gallop, the sheriff flat along the horse's back, his face almost buried in mane.

Knowing instinctively that he had run into three hardcases, he pressed the gelding unmercifully. There was no mistaking the brutal intent of the three riders; they were on a diagonal track, moving down the incline and by the time they positioned behind him they would be uncomfortably close. Even as he spurred the gelding, a shot cracked from an eager gun. The slug was a long way from doing any harm, but its whistle as it cut the air was real enough.

'Damn! Turtle Back hombres!' was Joe Clark's bitter thought and he cursed his luck. He had not expected this.

A law-badge was sometimes no protection; rather the reverse – it provoked hate. He had been recognised, of course. Flinging a backward glance, he saw the huge fat man, astride his cayuse like some ungainly monster, and thought he had seen him once before. The man was hanging on to his grey top hat with one hand and holding the reins with expert horsemanship.

They had cut yards off the distance between them

and were gaining. Evidently they had fairly fresh animals. His own had had the spunk taken out of it by the last few hours of riding.

Another shot winged like a vicious dart above his head, the bark of the gun too close for comfort. He swore angrily. Did they intend to gun him down, kill him? Were they just three murderous animals, ready to kill simply because they knew he stood for law?

The gelding's neck was outstretched and nostrils wide with communicated fear. Joe Clark felt the cold touch of fear, sure enough. He had never professed to be a hero; just a man doing a job – he had said that often enough to Rod Kane. He was a man who wanted to live. A wife depended on him, loved him, was eager to see him at the end of each day, yet knowing all this he had never knowingly backed away from danger, and the gun he packed was no ornament. He had killed with it.

Fury chased the coldness out of his gut. Anger that he should be hunted like some damned coyote. And, in anger, he heaved his Colt from his holster. In another second he swerved his horse sharply to the right, feeling the animal's hooves dig frantically at loose bits of grass and dirt; feeling the ribbed barrel of the animal's chest strain for balance.

The swift jerk to the right was a good trick. For some moments he was parallel to the forward motion of the three riders and he could see them clearly. He had no time to lose.

He whipped down the left side of the horse, with

58

only one foot in the stirrup. The other leg was hooked over the animal's rump. To the on-coming riders he had ceased to be a black blotch of a target; he had disappeared. They could see only an empty saddle.

In a second his gun poked over that same empty saddle and barked. He had three head-on targets, for moments only. There were just enough split seconds in which to aim before the other riders wheeled their mounts also.

As he emptied the gun, he saw luck had favoured him. One of the lean riders jerked as if speared. His hands covered his face and blood spurted.

Joe Clark swung back to the saddle. He could not hang on any longer. The old Injun trick had served a purpose. He dug spurs at the animal and it stretched into a new burst of speed.

The sheriff glanced back and saw that the rider he had hit had toppled from his saddle and was being dragged along by one foot in a tangled stirrup. The body raised a cloud of dust but braked the quivering horse.

The big beefy man and his companion were not deterred by the fate of their friend, for they attempted to close in again. Hooves beat a rapid tattoo on dry earth. They sent off a number of shots at the sheriff, the big man bellowing some lurid threats in a voice that could carry hundreds of yards.

For a moment Joe Clark thought he might get clear. Then he saw the tree-covered mound of earth towards which the horse was rushing and luck deserted him.

The slug dug a furrow along the right-hand side of his pulled-down hat, burning and possibly deflecting in a grim moment of contact. All he knew was the utterly fast streak of pain and then the blackness which rushed up from some pit to engulf him.

Sheriff Joe Clark toppled slowly from his horse, like some dummy. He hit the ground hard and rolled over twice with sheer momentum and finally sprawled. His gelding ran on, free and scared, swerving in a wide circle as a riderless horse will do.

Sam Hadfield and his partner, Mick, drew up their panting cayuses, wheeled them, steadied them with brutal tugs at the leathers and a number of oaths. They jerked the animals closer to the prone sheriff.

'You reckon he's dead?' snarled Mick.

'He looks like a corpse but from the saddle I can't be sure, my man,' came the other's fruity voice. 'I suggest you jump down and investigate.'

'Why in hell? I'll just put another bullet through him ...'

'That would finalise it,' admitted Sam Hadfield.

'Waal, do I do it?'

'No. I've a feeling this man is the lucky kind. Dismount and turn him over.'

The man looked like objecting.

'I would, but my weight majestic though it is, advises me to stay in the saddle. You are the lean type, hombre. You will do as I say.'

The contempt in Sam Hadfield's rich tones did not penetrate the thick hide of the man, although he knew he was being ordered around. Muttering some-thing under his breath he climbed down from his saddle and, going towards the body of the sheriff, he turned him over with a rough heave. He stared at the red furrow in the side of Joe Clark's head for some moments and then felt inside the sheriff's shirt.

A minute later he jerked to his feet. 'This goldarn swine is still alive.'

'You know, my hunches are pretty smart,' mused Sam Hadfield. 'Alive, huh?'

'Yeah – the dirty badge-toter. And it sure looks like Nat …'

'I'm afraid you are right,' said the big man glancing back. 'He has only half a face and there is enough blood to sicken a horse slaughter man.'

'I'll give this jasper his finish!' raged Mick.

He raised his gun and his finger trembled on the curved trigger when Sam Hadfield's voice cut the air in an authoritative bark.

'No! We'll keep him alive. He'll be useful …'

6

Lawman's Revenge

It was late that day when the door of the sheriff's office opened roughly and Dirk Jordan strode in, a grin on his bearded face. He surveyed Rod Kane with his deep-set eyes, enjoying some superiority. Rod looked up from the desk where more paper-work had landed and stiffened when he saw the other man. His hand hovered near his gun butt.

'What do you want?'

'I got a little message for you, Deputy.'

'Message? About what?'

'About your boss – Sheriff Joe Clark. You don't know it, but he's met with a kinda accident.'

'What's happened?' Rod jerked to his feet. 'What the blazes are you getting at? I haven't forgotten you – and that side-kick of yours,' warned Rod Kane. 'Start talkin' or maybe I'll take a poke at you right now. What's all this about the sheriff?'

'Take it easy.'

Rod grabbed the man's vest. 'Talk! What's it all about? You come here jest to fool around?'

Dirk Jordan knocked the hands away. His amusement vanished. 'You've got work to do, Deputy. You've got to ride out to the Juana Ranch and tell old man John Lopez that his pal the sheriff is kinda tied up in Turtle Back with an ornery cuss named Sam Hadfield and if he wants the sheriff to go on enjoying living, the price will be five hundred head of prime beef.'

Rod Kane half lifted his gun from its holster and then allowed it to drop back again.

'All right – give me the details,' he said grimly. 'How come you get the job of contacting me? Where do you fit in?'

'Me? Waal, I'm kinda known in Turtle Back and it so happens I rode out there today. And who should I meet but my old pal, Sam Hadfield. He knows he can trust me so he gives me this little job to do. Seems like they met up with the sheriff somewhere near the trail to Turtle Back – only the badge-toter was a-goin' to the Juana Ranch to see his great friend, Senor John Lopez. The sheriff didn't make it.' Dirk paused, enjoying the opportunity to torment. 'There was a little gun-play an' the sheriff hit the dust with a head wound …'

'He's wounded? Badly?'

'Nope. He'll live – which is more than can be said for Nat Somers. He's sure dead! Waal, anyways, that ain't of no account – point is if John Lopez has any regard for his old pal the price is five hundred head.

And you've got the job of telling the wily old Mex all this ...'

'Why don't you volunteer?' snapped Rod Kane. 'Those punchers out there might welcome the chance to tear you into little bits ...'

'They might,' conceded the other. 'An' that's why you have got the job, Deputy. Anythin' else you want to know?'

'What happens if I take a posse into Turtle Back?'

'You won't. Because the sheriff would end up mighty dead.'

'This Sam Hadfield wouldn't get five hundred steers if he kills the sheriff.'

'Sure. It cuts two ways. But Sam figgers you'll ride to the Juana Ranch an' spill the tale to old Lopez. Sam says he thinks a lot of Joe Clark and will cough up. It's better than rustlin',' Dirk Jordan laughed.

'So this Sam Hadfield has been behind the recent spate of rustling?'

'Did I say that? Waal, maybe! Maybe! Who knows?'

'I'd like to meet up with this Hadfield hellion'

'You might,' said Dirk Jordan airily, 'if you help out in the drive of five hundred head to Turtle Back. Just to give you all details, Deputy – you an' Lopez have got two days to fix this deal up. Any foolin' around and Joe Clark gets a hole in the head.'

Rod tensed, glaring at the other. 'The cattle have to be driven to Turtle Back?'

'Yeah. Somewheres near the dump Sam Hadfield and some boys will take over – an' the sheriff will be sent out on his hoss. That's the deal. Neat, huh? I'm in on it – me bein' a pal of Sam Hadfield.'

'You get paid for your little efforts?' murmured Rod Kane.

'Sure do.'

'Well, add this to your account!'

Rod Kane's fists rammed out with all the anger the other man had generated behind them. He easily caught Dirk Jordan off guard. The right fist crashed into the man's chin, sending him staggering back. Rod's left followed up – as he took two steps forward – and hammered into the man's eye. There was savage satisfaction in hitting this man, not only on Joe Clark's account, but in memory of the punishment he and the other fellow had handed out to a trail-weary rider. Rod remembered the blows he had taken the other night. He crashed another right into Dirk's face, saw blood spurt from a damaged nose. He laughed grimly at the sight of this. Dirk took sudden fright, swung for the door and grabbed the handle.

Gone was his bravado when he was part of a two in one beat up. The door was exit. He managed to get through and out on to the boardwalk outside. Rod Kane followed, a sombre determination to hit this man again and again filling his stomach. There was, he figured, nothing to lose. If it was true that Joe Clark was held captive – and the yarn must have solid backing – then Dirk Jordan was only a minor individual in the scheme and slamming him to the ground would add no further harm to the sheriff.

So he followed the man outside and hit again and again until the hellion was staggering and bloodied. The man did try to fight back, but he had lost the initiative. Finally he was able to lurch away, cursing, mouthing threats and trying to stop the blood pouring from his damaged nose.

'Git!' snarled Rod. 'Git back to Hadfield and tell him I got the message! Git – afore I half-kill you! And one thing – if anything happens to Joe Clark I'll personally gun-hound everyone responsible if it takes me a year to do it!'

As Dirk Jordan staggered away to his horse, with some men watching cautiously, Rod stamped back to the office and ran his hands through a bucket of cold water.

Calming down, he knew he had work to do. Outside, the sun was sinking on the horizon, sending splinters of red and gold into the sky like a magic fan.

He would have to ride out to the Juana Ranch that night. It was not an easy chore to round up five hundred head of cattle and deliver them. This would take time.

He paused, drying his hands. It occurred to him that John Lopez was being called upon to pay a stiff price for his friendship with the sheriff. It was kidnap and blackmail. What if John Lopez refused?

On second thoughts this did not seem likely. John Lopez was a great man, wise and rich and understanding, knowing that money was not more important than life.

Rod Kane had an arduous night ride ahead of him, but first he would have to see Muriel Clark.

He went along to the neat little bungalow, trudging the busy street with the false-front hotels, seeing the riders entering town for the night. The sun sank lower over the hills, causing the cattle to bunch protectively in the many valleys that radiated for scores of square miles from the town. In the really distant hills, wild horses nudged close to each other. On the ridges, coyotes slunk belly to ground and sniffed for sign of the rising moon.

He knew he'd have a tough ride that night, but he couldn't waste time in mere sleep.

He came to the sheriff's little home, the place his wife insisted he maintained against the frequent practice of sleeping in built-on quarters at the back of the sheriff's office. Rod straightened his shoulders, knowing the brief little talk was not going to be pleasant, but was something he owed to Muriel Clark. He would tell her not to worry too much – a trite assurance for a woman who worried all the time about her man.

Long Haired Jim North had spent the day prowling around Cactus Plain, watching the riders hitch their mounts to the tie-rails, scanning the men on the streets. He did not expect to find the man he sought among the Irish labourers who had tramped miles from the distant railroad workings just for a night's booze in the town. Nor did he anticipate seeing the notorious Gideon James working as a mule skinner. If he frequented a saloon, it would be as a customer. Maybe he was booked in at one of the three hotels, living the life of Riley on the stolen gold. There had been enough value in those nuggets to set up two men.

Jim North was more annoyed about the fact of being robbed after all that blamed digging, than he was concerned about the money. He had never been a man to set great store by money. As long as he had food, a good horse and a rifle, he was happy. Still, he had located the gold in those durned mountains and worked long hours to get it out. He had been wronged, and a bull-like stubbornness about the elusive badman possessed him.

He also hugged to himself a cynical delight that he had become so adept at handling that pearl-butted gun. He swore that there was magic in that gun. It was no ordinary Colt. It wasn't just the handle and the notches. There was something he could not explain – a feeling that the spirit of the elusive outlaw was behind that hogleg every time he drew it from leather.

How else could his new-found speed with a gun be explained? He had never been a gunman, but now his hand was faster than a sidewinder's strike – and it wasn't just because he had practised such a lot in the last few weeks. Nope! There was a wicked agility in the gun of Gideon James – and it would be the end of the jasper himself!

First, he had to meet up with the devil. Maybe that bald-headed little cuss was wrong about Gideon James being in Cactus Plain. But he had seemed all-fired sure. This town could be just another fizzle – like Danby and Dry Sands. All the same, he'd mosey around supposing he spent another year on tracking down the man. All he needed was a sight of the black-bearded, black-haired, blue eyed rat.

Long Haired Jim sauntered along the boardwalk, noted the dying sun and wondered if he should spend the night in the barn along with his horse. If he figured to get into a hotel they were so dad-blamed particular they would want him to wash – and maybe buy a new shirt. A bed wasn't worth all that fussing and fretting.

Then Long Haired Jim saw the deputy ride by on his big black horse, his deerskin vest flapping with the movement of the big animal's haunches. Rider and man were moving swiftly, as if filled with purpose. A rifle angled into the saddle holster. A coiled rope and water canteen hung around the saddle pommel.

'Hey, Deputy, you goin' somewheres?' Long Haired Jim called out.

Rod Kane reined and stared at the skinny figure in the disreputable clothes. 'You, amigo! Still looking?'

'Yep. You seem hell-bent.'

'I'm riding out to the Juana Ranch,' said Rod briefly.

'Is that so? That's the big spread, huh? Turtle Back is 'way out thataways, ain't it?'

'A long way past the Juana Ranch …'

'Wonder if I'd meet up with Gideon James out thataway? More likely he's holed up in Turtle Back than this durned town. Say, ain't it a bit late to be hitting the trail? If that cayuse sticks a leg in a hole, you could be thrown.'

'I'll have to chance that,' rapped the deputy. '*Adios.*'

Long Haired Jim grinned. 'So long! See you around!'

As Rod Kane urged his big black on, Jim North turned and slouched along the road, still grinning. Damned if he didn't like that young deputy; there was a man you could trust with your last dollar.

He turned past a dark alley, stepped on to the boardwalk that led past The Imperial where yellow lamplight spilled from windows that were not yet shuttered. Unlike the Last Chance saloon, which was favoured by any wandering range man, The Imperial attracted a better class of customer and was partly a hotel. While gaming went on in small comfortable rooms, there was no noisy piano thumping out old war tunes. The Imperial was visited by men of substance and the black store suit and gold watch-chain were more in evidence than sheepskin chaps and Colts.

As Long Haired Jim trundled along he was quite oblivious to the tall man standing in a dark patch near The Imperial entrance. The man watched the shabby drifter, turning his head slowly as Jim North went past. He followed North's progress thoughtfully with a long stare until the wanderer turned a corner and disappeared.

Then Al Smith swivelled and, confident, smiling,

walked into the bright interior of the hotel and headed for the select room where he ordered Old Grant's whisky.

It was nearly midnight when Rod Kane turned a tired horse into the courtyard around the Juana Ranch. A lookout near the gate came forward inquiringly and white teeth grinned when Rod was recognised. The young man took the deputy's horse away for water and feed, and, moments later, Rod was talking to John Lopez. The tall man with grey curled hair listened to Rod in mounting anger. His moustache bristled and his body stiffened angrily inside his fine velvet cord suit.

'They have done this to my friend, Joe Clark! They would murder him! These scoundrels should be wiped out and that confounded owlhoot town razed to the ground! Why I've a good mind to get my men and ride out – now!'

'Hold it, Mr Lopez.' Rod glanced tautly around the fine, large room but he did not see the lavish furnishings and the huge stone fireplace, the Mexican art and Indian rugs, rather his eyes were unseeing and troubled. 'You know what would happen. They'd hear riders coming a mile away and kill Joe Clark out of sheer spite. Life is nothing to these hellions …'

'Of course. I spoke in anger, Senor Kane.' John Lopez took a deep breath. 'I will have to pay the ransom. Damn these rustlers! They've been at my cattle for months – and now this.'

'Five hundred head is a lot,' muttered Rod.

'But I will not hesitate. To me, men like Joe Clark are beyond price. The people of Cactus Plain pin a badge on him and slap him on the back, but that is all too easy for some. I will gladly pay for the sheriff's freedom – but we must be sure we are not to be tricked.'

'I could try to sneak into Turtle Back – maybe tonight.'

John Lopez spread his hands. 'But the risk! One man – it is crazy.'

'It's a big loss of stock even for the Double J,' said Rod slowly.

'I don't begrudge the price. But I'll warn all possible buyers that they risk running foul of the law if they buy beef with my brand on it and no bill of sale from me.'

Rod Kane rode out again, tired and reflecting sombrely that this was a hard country and gave a man a lot of riding. Weariness, reflective thoughts and the monotonous jogging of his horse combined to make the youthful Kane drowsy, and so it was he became a victim to the two men who lay in wait for him.

They tore out of cover, with yells of triumph, and a rope whirled. It dropped around Rod Kane's shoulders and tightened in a second. Then the two men were on him. Swift movements robbed the deputy of his holstered gun. The man with the rope reined in his cayuse and heaved on the manila. Rod was tugged off his horse's back, landing with a painful thump on the grass ground.

'Ha, ha! Got him!' howled Bert Skinner, rope expert.

73

'I told you, Dirk, I was pretty nifty with a rope! Brought him low like a blamed steer ready for brandin'.'

'Maybe that's what we should do with the skunk!' snarled Dirk Jordan. 'I told you he'd be out this-away. He's been to the Juana Ranch – deliverin' the message.'

Within moments the unfortunate young Kane was suspended from the ground as they tossed the rope over a branch and hauled. Skinner ripped off his shirt as Dirk got a fire going underneath their victim. As Skinner heated the blade of his knife in the fire Kane kicked out with booted feet which gave his tormentors an idea. They tugged off his boots and positioned him so the flames began to lick at the bottoms of his feet, and the thick, damp wool socks began to smoulder. Rod felt his senses swim as a hundred stabs of pain streaked through his tortured soles.

'How's it feel, lawman?' Dirk asked him, grinning.

'He ain't in a talkin' mood,' chuckled Skinner, and they left him, dangling and struggling, well satisfied with their revenge.

Rod Kane was left there for a long time, which would have been longer still but for two ex-miners in a lumber wagon on a secretive night ride, on their way to meet up with two other rannies in the Shadow Mountains.

Dan Bale and Wally Hands came first across Rod's horse, and in looking for the rider, glimpsed in the shadows the limp, swaying, bootless man tied to the tree-branch. When they cut him down he fell in the dying embers of the fire beneath him.

They were tempted to leave him and take his horse, and get on their way with their load of mine shoring timber, but tossed Kane in the back of their wagon. Neither man was unkind, each was reluctant to leave the unconscious lawman in the wilds. They had to press on, so decided to do what they could for him and send him on his way, once he revived. They hoped this would be before dawn, so that no one else at their camp would know about it.

The problem solved itself for after arriving at the camp they left the deputy in the back of the wagon only to find him missing next morning.

7

Bootless Deputy

As the sun warmed the earth, the man in the cleft of rock and sandy shale felt his strength slowly return to his shocked body. Just to walk was a small torture yet he'd staggered from the wagon because he was living and that meant the urge to struggle and fight. He had raised himself, looked around in the faint light of a disappearing moon. He had seen the tents in the canyon, his horse hitched to the wagon tail-gate. Then he had stared up to the sky and the background of dark hills rising like rocky battlements and, hazily, he had wondered where he was, although something about the terrain reminded him he had seen it before.

And then he had gently lowered himself from the wagon and staggered away. Instinct told him to get away and hide. He reacted like an animal that was hurt; he found a hole and sank into it. He had reached this cleft of rock, partly over-hung with cholla cactus, just as his surge of strength ran out. He had to rest. He had to ... so he crawled into the cleft and hugged the earth, the cholla swinging back and almost covering his body.

And so he had lain for what seemed a long time, breathing deeply, swallowing, flexing muscles and even his fingers. He was just about to get up and go for his horse when he saw one of the sleeping men rise, stand and stretch for a moment and then walk to the wagon.

Rod Kane sank back, observing.

He was gunless. His rifle was still in the saddle holster. But the bulky man in the leather jerkin was moving to the wagon. Rod watched. The man seemed to stand stock still when he whipped back the blanket. He did not raise any alarm; instead he walked quickly around the perimeter of the camp, pausing to stare into gullies that ran like smooth tunnel-like fingers into the pileup of rocks rising out of the canyon.

He came quite close to where the deputy lay but he did not halt. He seemed to make up his mind that the man he sought had vanished. And then he did what seemed to be an odd thing to Rod's grimly observant eyes. The man unhitched the black horse. He did not touch the rifle or water canteen. He led the horse quietly away to the mouth of the canyon, a point a good five hundred yards distant, and then he slapped the horse away into the hazy sunlit morning. It seemed he desired to get rid of the animal. Probably he figured the cayuse would drift back to its home stable.

Rod Kane flattened, thinking many useless things.

When a man's eyes are only inches from the earth, the world contracts. He thinks of his pains and desperate ways of surviving. He wished he had his water bottle. Just to think about it made his throat seem like a monstrous lump of flesh that didn't belong to him. He wished to hell he was on the back of the horse. He even wished, for a few fleeting moments of weakness, that he was in bed and there was a woman tending him. Her face looked like June Latimer.

Rod Kane snapped himself out of his thoughts and raised himself. Maybe he could get away from here; pick up his horse. It struck him that some men had cut him down and brought him here. The unknown had done him no harm. Maybe they could help, if he walked back to that camp and get his horse again? Something – some sense of sombre caution – warned him not to chance it. Who were these men? There must be others in the tents. What were they doing here?

The sun began to climb, playing a gentle warmth on his back. He inched up again and stared at the camp. He gave a bitter exclamation when he noticed another man had stirred. The man ducked out of the tent and stood talking and yawning with the first man – the bulky one who had looked around for the missing body.

In the minutes that passed, Rod Kane lay like a burrowing animal, bitterly resenting this role, but knowing there was danger if he walked out and asked these men for help. He could not explain this bug in his mind; but it was there. Maybe it was a reaction from his grisly experience at the hands of Dirk Jordan and his side-kick; and maybe it was that and other little mental warnings.

There were four men in this camp. They were all up and about now, tending to chores. A fire was lit and the smell of bacon cooking came to Rod and honed his sense of hunger.

As the sun climbed above the hills, Rod spent some time considering the lay of the land. Judging by the position of the sun, and remembering where he had been jumped on the trail from the Juana Ranch, he came to the conclusion he was near the Shadow Mountains. He clinched the hunch when he cautiously turned around and stared at the high rocky peaks rising in bluish pinnacles only a few miles away.

Still uncertain of these four men, but knowing he had to get away, he watched them as they unloaded the wagon. He saw the timber and then the length of small gauge rail line, fastened with cross-pieces, and then the bogie with the iron wheels. Finally, he saw an old little man with unkempt grey hair carry three boxes clearly marked dynamite and set them down in a cave-like hole in the canyon wall.

All at once it dawned on Rod Kane. He remembered old Red Cloud's laconic comments about the white men in the Shadow Mountains; that they were searching for the lost mine where the treasure had been cached by frightened men all those many, many years ago. Sure, it added up. This was mining gear they had on that wagon; and he was near the Shadow Mountains area – that he was sure of now.

These men had no right to be on this land. It was just inside the Indian Reservation and was subject to State Orders. If the Indian Agent got to learn about this, he could call the troopers to clear the men off. These men must know all this and would be a bit wary. Although one of them had helped him – saved his life, in fact – they would not welcome a stranger, especially a deputy sheriff.

Time was passing and he was becoming stiff with the tension. He had to make some move. Maybe he would get the chance to escape pretty soon because the four men seemed to have work to do. They had retreated down the canyon and were probing a high rock face with pick-axes and spending some time jawing about what they should do.

Rod thought he might be able to creep away while their attention was occupied. Maybe he could find his horse; if the animal had found green grass to nibble it might not have gone far. He still figured it was strange that the man should turn the horse loose, almost as if he didn't want anyone to see it.

The men were poking at the rock face that towered above them for a hundred feet. It was yellowish sandstone, with a thick seam of reddish granite running parallel with the canyon floor. For years gold hunters had roamed around these hills, long before the Indians had been given the territory as a reservation. A hundred years ago, when the mission had been burnt and the padres killed, gold seekers had been digging out shafts and holing the earth like gophers for miles around the Shadow Mountains. Gold had been mined, but not in any great quantity and now there were only a few prospectors in the county.

But these men were not after natural veins or nuggets of gold. It seemed to add up that these were the galoots illegally searching the area for sign of the old shaft in which the padres had hidden their wealth. In those days the old Spanish Missions were not above garnering gold ornaments, silver and jewels to add to the glory of their establishments. As the story ran, this treasure was now hidden in some lost old mine shaft. Maybe it would never be found. The West had its share of these unlocatable treasure troves.

Rod Kane raised himself, tensed. The men were working, tapping experimentally at a rock face that had many discolourations. Maybe he could get away now.

He was poised when he heard the sound of an oncoming horse. The rider was somewhere around the edge of the canyon mouth, putting his mount to a fast trot. So there was another man! Rod sank back, cursing a bit at his luck.

He could not run for it because he could only move slowly and would surely encounter this new rider. He had to lie low again.

He waited for the newcomer to pass. He heard the hoof-beats and a shout from some of the men.

'Hi, boss! Take a look at this rock face!'

' 'Morning, boss!'

There were other greetings and the hoof-beats stopped. Rod judged the man was dismounting. Curious, he thought maybe a look at this man might be a good idea. It was actually a County affair, these men being up here in the Indian Reservation, and not the job of a sheriff or a deputy to warn them they were guilty of an offence in working land belonging strictly to the Mojaves. Still, he wondered who the blazes this man might be.

He cautiously looked out of the cleft which had been home for an hour and stared down the canyon at the group of men. As before, he did not know any of the four he had seen earlier. But he did recognise the newcomer.

A distinct physical shock jarred his already tensed nerves and body.

For the new arrival was no other than the smooth gunman, Al Smith. His confident face and blond hair were clearly visible.

Al Smith was the boss of these treasure seekers ... that was his reason for being in Cactus County. Was his status as a cattleman in Cimarron, Texas, a fake?

Dirk Jordan and Bert Skinner rode back swiftly to the sprawling frontier town and hit their grubby bedrolls in the one-roomed shack which lay behind some cattle pens. This was home to the two hellions. That it stank was not only due to the fact that it was adjacent to the cattle that were often penned there while awaiting buyers. The two men were not very particular, except when they wanted to prop up a bar counter and impress some pals. Then they would clean up and maybe put on a fresh shirt. The cabin was somewhere to sleep and meals could be cadged or, when in funds, obtained at the Chinese eat-house.

They slept soundly for the rest of the night, for they were men who did not dream. When they finally stirred, which was about mid-morning, they rolled cigarettes and smoked morosely and stared at each other with no interest. Then, with a grunt, Dirk Jordan indicated that he was going along to the Last Chance for an early drink.

'I'll be in the money inside the week,' he commented, 'so I'm spendin' now.'

'You figure Sam Hadfield will pay you?'

'Sure. I'll get a cut when he gets those beeves.'

'What about me? Ain't you goin' to fit me in?'

'Maybe. We'll see Sam later …'

They strolled to the street outside and lounged against a clapboard wall, staring at the surge of people and horses that the new day had brought. A small herd of cattle was driven down the street to the pens, wandering slowly, bawling. Within ten minutes the cattle were clear and then two wagon teams laden with corn rolled into town and stopped outside a chandler's.

'Waal, I'm a'goin' for that drink,' snapped Dirk Jordan. 'You? You got the price?'

'Ain't you a-goin' to stake me?'

'Aw, all right. Hell, you never have a dime! Now old Clay always had the price on him ...'

They were inside the Last Chance about an hour, steadily spending down to Dirk Jordan's last dollar and as a consequence becoming a little loose-tongued. Someone in the saloon made a reference to the sheriff being held hostage by Sam Hadfield in the outlaw town of Turtle Back.

'How the hell d'you know that?' Dirk Jordan swung on the man, an ageing assistant to the town blacksmith. The man was having an early drink of ale, having done a spell of hot work at the smithy.

'Plenty folks heard about it ...'

Dirk's deep-set eyes glared. 'Who's done the talkin'?'

'I dunno ... jest some feller's been yapping to a galoot fresh from Turtle Back. Seems to be true. The sheriff went ridin' to the Juana Ranch an' he ain't got back.'

'Nothin' in that ...'

'Nope, but I tell you the news is sure goin' around town ...'

Dirk and Bert Skinner grinned. 'Waal, what's a sheriff!' And Dirk downed his beer.

'What's a deputy, for that matter!' sneered Bert Skinner. 'Heh! Heh!' He laughed at the thought of Rod Kane.

Dirk flashed the other man a warning glance. But the young hellion felt insolently confident.

'You won't see the blamed deputy in a hurry!'

The man with the leather apron and smoke-begrimed face stared curiously at Bert Skinner. 'How come? What's wrong with the deputy? Should ha' thought he'd be out lookin' for the sheriff …'

'Well, he ain't!' sneered Bert Skinner. 'He won't be lookin' for …'

Dirk Jordan grabbed his arm and glared, hissing a warning. 'Shut your blamed mouth!'

'What the hell! I'll say what I want …'

'Ain't you got no savvy?' The two men exchanged ferocious glances. One was angry, fearful; the other openly sneering.

Then Bert Skinner drank his beer, slammed down the empty glass. 'Aw, what the heck d'you worry about? You worry too much, pardner … allus figurin' out angles … who cares about the deputy? Not me. Who cares about the goldarned sheriff, come to that!'

Dirk Jordan gripped his friend's arm and urged him away from the bar. They moved slowly to the batwings, arguing, slightly drunk.

The few men at the pine bar watched their departure with varying degrees of concern and curiosity. The elderly blacksmith's assistant attempted to finish his mug of ale. Two other men, range waddies by the look of their clothes, who were probably looking for jobs, began to debate the strange tale concerning the missing sheriff.

From that they went on to discuss other yarns of sheriffs they had known, in the way men have over a drink. It was, obviously, not their problem, and like people the world over, they shrugged it off. But the thin man in the corner had been listening to all the talk. He had been half-hidden behind a partition that made a neat alcove of the corner, for those customers who wanted some privacy from the main bar, and he had seen Dirk Jordan and his pard in a mirror in the alcoved corner.

But Long Haired Jim came out when the two had gone. He did not want another run-in with the ornery cuss with the deep-set eyes; he had pulled Gideon James' gun on the man and the galoot did not like it. There was no percentage in looking for trouble. He just wanted to locate Gideon James – that was all. But at the same time, the few remarks he had overheard about the deputy had aroused his curiosity.

He liked Rod Kane.

Jim North approached the man in the blacksmith's apron. 'Say, friend, what's all this about the sheriff? I didn't quite hear all you said. What's the details?'

'Details?' The other man studied Long Haired Jim for a second and decided he was harmless. 'Why just what I heard. Seems like Sheriff Joe Clark is being held by some blamed outlaws in that pesky Turtle Back an' they want a whole herd of cattle from John Lopez for his release. That's more or less what I heard, friend.'

'That's a darned disgrace.'

'It is,' agreed the other. 'An honest man ain't safe around here – I've always said that. I kinda liked Joe Clark ... always had a word with me.'

'Those two rannies – you heard what they said about the deputy. Did that make sense to you?'

'Nope. Just shootin' off at the mouth, I guess …'

Long Haired Jim shook his head slowly. 'Not so sure. That older feller didn't like his pal talkin' so much. Now I heard him say that you won't see the deputy again …'

'Yeah … I got that. Don't make much sense – unless that young feller has run into trouble as well …'

'Now that could be.' Jim North nodded his head and pushed back his battered hat.

'Well, I don't know anythin' about it.' The man in the apron made to go. 'Maybe he's tangled with the same lot that's got the sheriff. A nice state of affairs! Why, if I was a younger man I'd move on!'

And the man walked stiffly to the batwings, leaving Long Haired Jim to his thoughts.

He did not stay in the saloon. He had a restless feeling that maybe there was something he could do – and should do – to help a gent he liked. The longer he thought about it, the more certain he was that Rod Kane was in trouble.

Those two hombres who had yapped about the sheriff and the deputy knew some secrets. As for the Sheriff of Cactus Plain, it seemed clear in this case that the outlaws from Turtle Back had him. But what of the young deputy?

He recalled how he had seen Rod Kane riding out late last night and the deputy had said he was going to the Juana Ranch. He had not stated why he was hitting the trail at such a late hour.

'Figures to me he run into grief last night,' muttered Long Haired Jim. 'Now where? Somewheres along that trail to the Juana Ranch – the direction o' Turtle Back.'

The thin drifter in the shabby red shirt made up his mind. He'd ride out. Sometimes a man could nose around and discover things, even in a land so vast and empty as Cactus County. Anyway, he'd take a chance. He'd get his grey stallion.

He cantered out of the town less than ten minutes later, for Long Haired Jim was a man with simple possessions. He owned to a saddlebag with some grub in it, such as a can of beans, some jerky beef, flour and coffee. He had a water canteen that had been filled at some strange holes in its time. He had his rifle in the saddle holster and a bedroll – and, of course, the pearl-handled gun.

'Reckon I oughta been a rich feller by now,' he mused as he rode along. 'Me – with all that gold! Reckon I could ha' been living like a lord – whisky and gals – yessir! Not like a desert bum – nope! And all on account o' that durned night rider – Gideon James. Reckon he's takin' his ease by now – on my gold!'

He recalled how he had worked for the yellow stuff – digging, sifting rock, sand and rubble to find the infrequent nugget. Hours and weeks of arduous work under a hot sun. He had spent weeks looking for the claim, after he had got the hunch that there was gold in that rocky area of the Little Horn. A lot of darned work – for nothing.

'Me – I oughta be a rich man!' he snorted. 'I should ha' been a gent!' He got out his baccy and chewed. 'I ain't always been a low-down drifter. I remember when I had a job – now when was that? Aw, it was a long time ago – never mind.'

He worked himself up into a fine mood of indignation. On many long rides he had spent hours ruminating like this. It kept him going, kept him searching for the elusive Gideon James. His weird dreams of what he could have done with the vanished wealth were, in a sense, just as satisfying as possessing the gold itself.

The heat of the day brought out greasy sweat down his cheeks and neck and frequently he mopped up with his dirty neckerchief. Once he saw some riders cutting through a valley but he judged them to be ranch-hands out on some expedition. Then he skirted gentle slopes where herds of longhorns grazed. He rode on, a trifle bemused, wondering just what he expected to find, if anything. This was a big country and a valley ridge could hide a man and a horse easily. At the same time, a high point of land afforded a view for miles around.

Twice he had climbed to a ridge and scanned the terrain. He knew he was near the Double J brand land, from the information he had picked up in Cactus Plain, and if he kept on long enough he'd get near the outlaw town, Turtle Back. Maybe he should ride for that place? Maybe he'd pick up sign of Gideon James out there? A man never knew. Some day his moseying around would pay off.

Long Haired Jim stopped to drink water and he gave some to his grey stallion. He would let the horse drink its fill at the next spring they encountered. He recorked the canteen and jigged the horse on.

Maybe if he drifted into Turtle Back he could listen to the rumours about the sheriff. Sure, it was none of his business but maybe he could nose around and observe things. A man could figure out a lot by just watching and listening. Strangers apparently rode into the outlaw town and stayed without question as long as they 'fitted'. It wasn't the place for an obviously responsible person, but, then, he didn't look like a man of property. He would be watched but that was all. He had been in these shabby communities before without coming to harm.

Long Haired Jim rode to the top of another ridge and then stood in the stirrups and, shading his eyes, stared all around him. The silent land shimmered with heat haze and little wind stirred. Ahead stretched rock-girt valleys studded with bunch-grass and odd clumps of cedar trees and oaks. Then right ahead in the distance were the bluish hills of the Shadow Mountains, the border land to the Mojave Reservation. Sure, it was a great wide country, with the wandering herds of longhorns and the odd rattler in the rocky crevices.

Then he saw the lone rider, moving on a handsome

horse at a fast lope, as if the animal had all the stamina in the world. Jim North rode down from the ridge at once, with the instinct of a man who had ridden lonely trails and did not want to be noticed until he was ready.

The other rider cut through the valley, his horse's hooves kicking up a tidy dust. He was making a fast ride to some particular place, that was for sure.

Then Jim North got out his trusty spy-glass and took a good look at the rider.

He saw the fine silk shirt and some other details. The man wore a new stetson and one gun. He rode as if he had been born to horsemanship, a confident rider.

'Sure is makin' a good turn o' speed on that critter,' muttered Jim North. 'Now where's he headin'?'

He decided to tail the rider for some distance. After all he was out moseying around, the man was a stranger, he had not seen him before. Had he left Cactus Plain? It seemed like it.

Long Haired Jim pushed his grey stallion on, wishing he could get real close to the other rider so that he could see his face. But maybe that would be an unwise move, this territory was full of ornery cusses who shot first and asked questions later. Better to spy on the galoot. Anyway there was no other rider for miles around. Just where the heck was this jasper heading? He was in an all-fired hurry, that was sure.

After three miles of trotting after the other range rider, cutting through small ravines and valleys in order to avoid being seen, Long Haired Jim came to the conclusion that the man was not heading for Turtle Back.

He was taking a different bearing over the land. And he was not bound for the Juana Ranch, it seemed. He was off that trail.

So just where was he going?

He kept on the other's tail for some miles, obeying some hunting instinct, some feeling that this man was on an unorthodox errand. And then, slowly, the hunch hardened.

The man was bound for the Shadow Mountains.

Well, maybe he was starting some long ride that would take him right out of the territory? But why by way of the Shadow Mountains? That was forbidden land to a white man, under the Mojave Treaty, and it was the road to nowhere, in any case.

Jim North had the sense to know that a wise range rider knows when he is being trailed. So he kept his distance and in the end this caution lost him his man. Long Haired Jim breasted a rise expecting to see the man still loping along the valley floor – but when he stared down there was no movement. Nothing stirred, no black shadow went galloping over the huge expanse of sun-baked land. He listened. No sound drifted to his ears, only the silence eternal to these hills and valleys.

So he had lost the man. By now he must be down in another valley, having skirted the base of the hills. Jim North slipped down from horse and flattened to the ground, his ear straining for any vibration that indicated a horse's hooves. But the ground gave no clue. Like the air around, it was silent.

'Tarnation! I done lost him! Waal, maybe that jasper was of no account...'

He remounted. The horse wandered on and found a spring of water bubbling from some depth in the wide, lonely land, and the animal would not be urged away until it had had its fill. Jim North thought he was becoming kind of hungry because so far the only nourishment he'd had had been beer in the Last Chance saloon. Maybe he ought to stop wandering and fill his belly. As for the lone rider on the handsome horse, he had disappeared, intent upon his own business, whatever that might be.

So he was not far from the Shadow Mountains, standing high and blue in the distance. By all accounts few white men had been inside the territory for many a year. In those hills the Mojaves lived, brooding, perhaps, on past glories.

'Goshdarn it, I'm jest wanderin',' North muttered. 'Still I'd know that rider again – if I saw him. Maybe I won't ...'

It was almost too much to believe when he saw the riderless horse on the grassy gradient, a place where the rain evidently collected and produced the green grass tufts.

As Long Haired Jim rode up, the horse lifted its head and whickered a greeting.

He stared at the black, at the coiled rope and the

rifle snug in the saddle holster and right away he recognised the horse – the black that Rod Kane had ridden out of town; there was no mistake about it.

But where was the deputy?

8

Mystery Gunman

Rod Kane stared grimly at the bunch of men down the canyon. Al Smith was there and they were pointing at the rock face, arguing. One man stabbed with a pick-axe and then desisted. Apparently there was some disagreement about the matter in hand. Rod narrowed his eyes and thought they were on a crazy quest, trying to find the old mine shaft. Many men had tried. Every so many years some optimist prospected around until his time or money or energy ran out.

Strangely, he would have thought that Al Smith was not the type to waste his energy on impossible ventures. Had the man some new knowledge concerning the lost treasure, the so-called La Mina Del Padre? Who the devil was the man, anyway? A cattleman taking time off to go treasure seeking!

Rod remembered the telegram he had sent to

Cimarron. Maybe there would be a reply shedding some light on the man.

The urgent need was to get out of this damned crack in the rocks. He had been there so long cowering, he felt like some damned sidewinder. He had to get out, make a break for it. And now seemed the best chance, with the bunch of men busy down the sandy canyon.

He had to get clear of them. It was no use appealing to them to help. For a start they were unknown characters and they were engaged in a shady venture in any case – and he represented the law.

He eased up for about the fourth time, but this moment was just right. Crouching low, making as little noise as possible, he ran lightly, carefully, for the canyon mouth. As he whipped around the straggle of boulders that marked the turning point, he looked back. The men were still busy. He had not been observed. Then he was running again, concealed by the rocks. He headed down the flat land, his ruined socks flapping, stumbling after he had covered a few hundred yards, wishing he had his boots. He flung a backward glance. Still no sign of pursuit.

Even so he knew full well the grim prospect before him. He was miles from anywhere. His horse might have wandered far away. He was still suffering from shock, with his breath rasping down a throat that felt like a red-hot chimney. Maybe there was a galoot whom he should thank – the man who had cut him down. One of those treasure seekers! But the strange business of shying his horse away needed some explanation. And he was sure nothing had been said to Al Smith when the man had ridden up. He'd watched for reaction from the man, but there was nothing. They had just set about their work, five men with work to do.

The flat semi-arid plain stretched before him for miles, a place of tufted grasses, sand and shale, now hot with the midday sun. The physical shock to his body, the hours of unconsciousness had taken a toll. As he moved along the flat, his pace slowed from a scrambling run to a staggering gait. The small hills ahead that indicated the broken land where the valleys held water and grass were still a long way off, it seemed, and no sign of his horse.

He slowed, plodded on uncertainly, lured to the round gentle hills that seemed to suggest cover where he might lie down and rest. He just had to get off his bare feet, away from the heat and the certainty that he could be spotted a long way back. If he could reach some hollow where there was water, he could rest. Maybe his strength would return. If he could find something to eat – fruits, berries – he might be able to walk on and on. If he got his bearings he could head in the direction of the Juana Ranch, hoping a wandering waddy might spot him.

Rod Kane stumbled on for about five miles, an exhausted man, dogged, holding on to his willpower, his desire to stay alive. Slowly the flat receded and small gullies split the land. He staggered along, noting the grass was sprouting in thicker clumps and definitely greener. There must be moisture in the ground. The sun hit his head with merciless heat and his brow felt like that of a man with a raging fever. He was hatless, having lost it long ago. He couldn't recall where or when his hat had gone – maybe when those two skunks had strung him up. A hat was almost necessity in this land. Heat shimmered up from the patches of sand and shale.

He found a thin trickle of water in a cleft of some reddish rocks and he bent his head to drink. The fluid eased the thickness of his tongue and his inflamed throat. He sank down on the grass and rested.

Almost an hour passed before he aroused himself. There was danger in resting too long, in sinking into a numb feeling where nothing mattered. He had to go on.

He drank once more before setting off, feeling the red water sink into his very tissues. He walked on, a little steadier after the rest. He climbed a hillock now that he felt stronger and stared around the broken terrain, judging his position. He was a long way off the recognised trails; a man without a horse, a man temporarily in poor physical shape.

He went on and began to stumble again. His head ached and his eyes blurred. He knew that this land could beat him; could mock at him as he wasted his strength in trying to traverse its seemingly unending miles. This land had taken many a life: men who had ventured into the maw of limitless lands and lost a horse or water.

He would have to rest again. In time hunger would strike at him although he felt he could tighten his belt for another twenty-four hours. He was just plain tired ... he needed to lie down ... he was already suffering from delusions ... because right ahead there was a man ... and two horses ...

A man ... and two horses ... a man on horseback ... surely ... was it a mirage created by heat and a terrible headache?

When the man shouted, he was still not sure. Then hands grasped him after he had stumbled headlong and fallen flat on his face – hands that gripped his shoulders and a voice that jerked out rough words of assurance.

'Hey there! You'll be all right, young feller – jest you rest awhile. Long Haired Jim will see to you. Goshdarn it, what in hell have they done to you?'

Rod Kane came out of his delirium some hours later to see the man in the faded red shirt making coffee and beans over a low fire he had lit with bits of brushwood. The flames of the small fire brought back painful memories.

Rod stared for some time. Then: 'Long Haired Jim!' It was an exclamation of relief as much as it was a greeting.

'Sure is me!' The drifter with the lank black hair grinned back. 'Hey, now, maybe you're ready to eat, huh?'

'I'd – sure – like – to – try –' Speech was a croaking vibration that rasped his throat.

'Hell, I can see you ain't in much shape to make speeches,' said Jim North. 'So don't you worry none.'

'They – dangled me – on – a rope!' muttered Rod. 'Those two – Dirk Jordan an' his – sidekick—'

'Don't try explainin'. I can guess most of it. It figures with what I heard at the Last Chance. Them blamed hellions!'

Rod nodded. Talking was too much trouble. The smell of beans came enticingly to his nostrils and he beckoned to Jim North to hand him some. He did not ask why the wanderer was out here; that was so much unessential talk. He tried the beans. They slid down his throat but it was a painful process. Still, he knew he had to get something solid down into his stomach. He looked up at his tethered black horse with a deep sense of satisfaction and gratitude. The black seemed a wonderful sight, complete with rifle and saddle.

'You should see a doc,' said Long Haired Jim suddenly.

Rod nodded; attempted some speech. 'Maybe … I need a man I can trust … feller who'll ride an' take messages …'

'You can count on me,' said the long haired man at once.

Rod smiled faintly. 'I've got to get back to town … see a doc … maybe get the swelling down … an' I figure I ought to let John Lopez know I won't be … at the Juana Ranch today …'

102

'I'll do the ridin',' said Jim North. 'I got reasons for moseyin' around, as you know, an' this is just my line. Yessir, you an' me got the same friends an' enemies. Them two hellions ain't fit to live with decent men – an' maybe I'll try this gun on them the next time we meet.' Jim North touched the pearl-butted .45 significantly.

'You'd pick a fight?'

'Yep – I've kinda taken a dislike to them rats.'

'I'd better tell you ... all that's happened to me ...' Rod croaked. And the laboured explanations came slowly. He told Long Haired Jim about seeing Al Smith in the canyon; the news about the men searching for the lost treasure; how Al Smith did not fit the part of visiting rancher.

'He ain't here on cattle buyin' business ... because I was told he'd never been near the Cattlemen's Association ... an' he looks more like a gunny ... than anythin' else ... now I know he's bossing that outfit of treasure seekers ...'

'That must ha' been the rider that I saw earlier,' commented Jim North.

'You saw him?'

'Yep. Through my spyglass, too.'

'Wasn't there something about him – that struck you as familiar?' asked Rod Kane slowly, his gaze fixed thoughtfully on the ground.

'I didn't get a close look. Smart galoot, I'd say. Fine rider too.'

Rod nodded.

103

'Now let me tell you, Jim, about the sheriff. A no-account name of Sam Hadfield has him as hostage somewhere in Turtle Back an' the price is five hundred head of cattle. Seems this man has been rustling Double J beef and has a market – and this little trick is an extension of that.' Rod gave the long haired man the details. 'John Lopez is willing to pay in order to get Joe Clark back safely. From what I've been told, Joe has a head wound.'

Jim North doused the fire. He gathered up his few pots. 'I reckon we ought to move on. You ready to ride?'

'Yeah – let's go. I feel a lot better – thanks to you, Jim.'

They climbed to saddles. Rod patted the mane of his black, savouring the smell of horseflesh again, the ripple of sinew in that proud neck. It was as good as being reunited with a very special old friend – which was more or less true.

They set of at a canter, the animals fairly fresh. They put some miles behind them quickly, cutting over valleys and ridges to join the main trail to Cactus Plain.

After an hour of riding, when they had slowed the cayuses, Rod asked the other man; 'You still got your Wanted bill on Gideon James?'

'Sure have. I'll carry that till I die!'

'He's a dark-haired galoot, isn't he?'

'Who?'

'Gideon James. Dark-haired, bearded. Blue-eyed.'

'Sure. That's what it says ...'

'And you saw him – once?'

'That's right – when he stole my gold.'

'And you nicked his arm or wrist?'

'Yeah, reckon I did. Say, what's on your mind?'

'Just – ideas!' muttered Rod.

'Howsabout tellin' me them?'

'I will – after we hit Cactus Plain an' I get a reply from Cimarron.'

Long Haired Jim was no fool. His eyes glittered shrewdly. 'Ah, that Al Smith hombre! Why, you don't figure ...'

'Forget it,' interrupted Rod Kane.

'Why? You tell me why, *amigo* ...'

'Because Al Smith is blond – as fair-haired as a gal!' gritted Rod. 'Now let's git to Cactus Plain.'

9

Recovery

About five hundred steers travelled slowly along the flat main valley bed leading to Turtle Back, raising dust in the air and bellowing protestingly. Double J brand cowboys rode on the flanks of this herd. Some of them were Mexican vaqueros with their grass ropes coiled on the saddlehorn.

It was two days after Rod Kane had ridden out to John Lopez and told him about the ransom – two days of work, for the big herd had not been easy to round up in a short space of time. And Rod had not been able to do much for the doctor had made him lie in bed for twenty-four hours while his body recovered from the physical shock.

He had stayed at Muriel Clark's home. She had insisted upon looking after him, nursing him. The simple tasks of caring for a man had kept her from worrying herself sick during that twenty-four hours.

He had got the telegram from the operator at the agency. Lying in bed he had read it, slowly, two or

107

three times, wondering but having to accept the facts.

It seemed that Al Smith was indeed a rancher at Cimarron and that he was in fact tall, blond, blue-eyed, with a dark moustache. The Town Marshal's reply indicated that Al Smith was well-known as a well-dressed man and that he carried a Frontier Colt. Al Smith had set off alone for some destination. At the moment no one knew his whereabouts.

It was a long reply. It should have satisfied Rod Kane but for some queer reason it did not. The 'bug' in his mind remained. And that didn't make sense. He tried to reason that maybe he subconsciously disliked Al Smith because the man had been seen with June Latimer and was, in fact, becoming very friendly with her. Maybe that was right – he just didn't like the man.

Staying in bed was not to his liking and he was on his feet as soon as he could and had gone around to the office to find an old pair of boots and socks.

He had gotten a new hat – a black one that matched his horse, he told himself humorously. He had also fixed himself up with another Colt from the desk in the sheriff's office.

There were two troublesome prisoners in the cells when he let himself in; put there, apparently, by a leading citizen who had become irritated by the two men's drunken activities and marched them along on the end of a sixgun and locked them up The names of the two were Milligan and O'Brien.

Rod arranged for a man to feed them and then he

left. He was going past the little dress shop when June Latimer walked out to inspect her window dressing.

Rod stopped, took off his hat. 'Hello, June! I – I—'

'We have nothing to talk about …'

'You can't go on blaming me!' he burst out. 'Ask anyone – Clay had it coming!'

'You killed him!' The dark eyes flashed the accusation. Her whole body, clad in a simple gingham dress, trembled with her sudden anger.

'Might have been anybody,' he snapped. 'Clay had some lousy friends – and he made enemies faster than most. It's time you realised the truth, June.'

'I – I – don't want to talk about it …'

'We were good friends once,' he muttered. 'June – I remember we used to walk down to the old chapel – don't you remember?'

'It – it – seems a long time ago …'

'Goshdarn it, I walked you that way less than two weeks ago!'

'Two weeks can see a lot of – of changes,' she said, and lowered her gaze.

'Yeah, a galoot like Al Smith moseys along …' he ground out and then stopped.

It was on the tip of his tongue to snap out criticism about the man; tell her he knew he was involved in illegal activities over in the Shadow Mountains, but he cut that back in the nick of time. Maybe it was wiser to keep the knowledge to himself, because it was a matter for the law.

'You don't like him,' she said tartly.

'No.' He was on safe ground there.

'Why? He is a gentleman – is that the reason? I believe he even helped you when you were attacked …'

Well, she was a woman and not above taunting a man. He smiled ruefully. 'All right, June – we're apparently no longer friends. But I'll be back – a-calling for you some day when things are better.'

'Will you?' Her black eyes were cold. Her hair, dark as the raven, haloed a lovely face. He knew she wasn't always like this. She used to laugh and look up to him with flashing eyes, knowing how he felt about her, and happy to be with him. He had kissed her and she had not objected – rather the reverse.

'I'll be back,' he said again. 'I'll be here long after Al Smith has gone.'

With that cryptic remark he had left her and returned to the sheriff's home. He told Muriel Clark that he was riding out to the Juana Ranch before nightfall.

He knew that Dirk Jordan and his partner were not in town because Jim North had scouted around the two saloons and returned with that report. Most likely the two men were holed up in Turtle Back. They'd figure on a cut-in for their efforts. Maybe they had boasted by now of the way they'd taken care of the deputy – unless some unknown rider from Cactus Plain, sympathetic to the outlaw element, had already ridden over with the news that the deputy sheriff had been seen in the streets of the town.

Rod Kane had walked past The Imperial. He had

110

seen Al Smith enter the place, walking swiftly, intent on some matter, and the man had not seen him. Rod glanced up to the sun, estimating there was time yet before setting off for the Juana Ranch. He crossed the road, stepping past some children and hens playing in the dust. He found Long Haired Jim, as he expected, sitting in the barn cleaning harness.

'There's a man in The Imperial – name o' Al Smith. I reckon he's just got into town, judging by the dust on his boots. Now I'd like you to take a good look at that gentleman …'

The other man turned. He looked up from the floor. 'Are you still gettin' ideas about that feller?'

'Just go into The Imperial an' buy a drink – see if he's around. Take a careful look, and then come back and tell me if there's anything about him that you recognise.'

'According to that telegram you got Mister Al Smith is in the clear …'

'Sure. It adds up. Maybe it's just my low-down cunning mind, Jim. But do as I say. Put a clean shirt on – some of the gents that frequent The Imperial are a bit fussy.'

'Me? I ain't got a clean shirt!'

'Hell, go out an' buy one!' yelled Rod and, laughing, he handed Long Haired Jim some money.

'Gawd a'mighty – a new shirt jest to git a drink!' grumbled the saddlebum. 'So I got to take a look-see at this gent? Are you loco? You told me Al Smith is as blond as a two-year-old gal!'

111

'Just look at him.' Rod made for the door. 'Just figure out what he'd look like with a beard.'

And with that he was gone.

Nothing arose from Jim North's little snoop around. The Imperial, of course. He saw Rod later, in the sheriff's office, and gave his verdict.

'Goddarn it, you've gone and upset all my ideas about Gideon James ...'

'How come?'

'Waal, now I don't know what to think. Sure that galoot, Al Smith, is the same height an' he's a pretty smart dresser an' he's got blue eyes – but, hell, I could find a hundred jaspers just about anywhere who'd answer to that.'

'Was there anything about the man that struck you as familiar?'

Jim North shook his head glumly. 'Nope. He was standing at a bar in the best end o' that saloon and he was hatless – an' only a crazy galoot would figure he looked like Gideon James.'

Rod laughed curtly. 'The truth is, Jim, you only think you'd recognise Gideon James the moment you saw him. It's just a fantasy in your mind.'

'It ain't!'

Long Haired Jim sprang to the defence of his pet theory. 'I'd know that galoot! Sure as I breathe I'd know him. No man can tell me otherwise. I'd jest know it – here.' He thumped his breast.

'You've just said you don't know what to think.'

'That's because that hombre ain't Gideon James!'

112

roared the other. 'You're tryin' to fox me, Deputy! Damn an' blast, I'll know when I meet up with that varmint!'

Rod Kane laughed it all away. Maybe he was all mixed up too. What sort of evidence had he? None. Just vague hunches that could make him look a fool. He'd have to watch it.

And so he had ridden out to Juana Ranch and met old John Lopez again. The rancher shook him warmly by the hand. It was late at night and there was only time for a consoling drink of brandy and a talk before turning in for the night.

'We got the herd together – and it's meant hard work for my hands. Still, I've got a surprise cooking up for those damned outlaws.'

Rod looked at the rancher in surprise. 'What have you got in mind?'

'I've sent a special rider over to Fort Davis with a request for troopers to clear out Turtle Back.'

'Before we get Joe Clark clear?' Rod was alarmed.

'Nope. ' The rancher laughed grimly. 'I'm not such a fool, Rod. We get the sheriff back to safety, tend to his wounds, see that he's all right. Then the troopers can ride in – but I warn you, my man is not back yet with a reply. For all I know Colonel Cusack might not have the time nor men for the request.'

'It's a good idea,' said Rod. 'You could win back your herd that way.'

'I had thought of that.' The grey-moustached rancher swirled his brandy around in the glass. 'I like to win, Rod. I take badly to the notion of dirty rustlers taking over five hundred of my stock, but I'll pay up if there is any danger to Joe Clark. My friends come before money, Senor Kane.'

'Not every man would pay this price,' ventured Rod. He sat in a large old rocking chair before the great stone fireplace, an Indian rug beneath his feet. He planned to stay the night so that he could ride out with John Lopez, his ranch-hands and the herd. He wanted to see everything and be on the spot when Joe Clark was released.

'I am the biggest rancher in this County,' said John Lopez, 'and that means I have responsibilities, *amigo*.'

They talked for some time. About the state of law enforcement in Cactus Plain and the number of hard-cases who were in the town. Many things were discussed, and Rod Kane made reference to the men searching for the lost treasure of the padres and the man who was apparently the boss, Al Smith.

Rod no longer linked Al Smith with the gunman, Gideon James. For one thing, he wasn't sure – he still had to admit he could be harbouring a delusion.

'The treasure?' laughed John Lopez. 'But surely not, my friend! For years many men have looked for that old mine shaft – long before the Mojave Reservation was planned. Always these expeditions fail – there is no treasure.'

'Their activity is illegal, right now,' said Rod. 'This is a matter for the Indian Agent.'

John Lopez had laughed again. 'Let them sweat it

out. Maybe the story is without foundation, my friend. No one really knows. And if it was true, the mountains will keep the secret – as they have done now for a hundred years.'

Rod nodded ruefully. 'That's one way to look at it but ...' He did not add there were complicating factors, that Al Smith was supposed to be a reputable rancher from Cimarron. He said nothing of his tiny little nagging hunches – how could he? They were a bit of a delusion – maybe some of Long Haired Jim's ideas about Gideon James had rubbed off on him.

So he said nothing and went to bed, and the next day dawned with the usual cloudless sky and the reminder that they had stern work ahead. Everything was ready to drive out the herd from the small bottle-necked canyon two miles from the ranch-house in which the cattle had been temporarily corralled and guarded that night.

It would be late that day when the slowly moving herd got anywhere near Turtle Back. No one knew exactly what might happen. For instance, was Joe Clark fit and well?

10

Big Time Rustling

The four riders sat tall in the saddles of their horses on a high ridge and stared into the distance, over the vast semi-arid plain that stretched for miles below the hill on which they stood. They could see the swirl of dust, the faint movement of a mass on the horizon. They knew the ransom herd would pass this way because any other trail would be more difficult.

'Hah, it is an interesting sight, gentlemen! Five hundred head! Now this is better than stealing a couple of dozen steers and risking a cowboy's bullet in the process. What do you think, Mick?'

Mick, the long lean saddle-bred man, looked at Sam Hadfield without a smile because humour in his roving career was something he had done without.

'Hope it comes off all right.'

'They will leave the herd when we tell them,' said

the huge man, his smooth face smiling under his absurd top hat. 'When the cattle get near these hills, you will ride out and inform them of my orders. They will let the herd settle and then ride west to the butte. Our friend, Dirk, here, will meet them and hand over the sheriff.'

Mick rubbed an unshaven face. He was thinking that he was exposed to danger and that the whole blamed set-up could misfire. Sam Hadfield seemed damned confident – but then he had a fast horse if anything went wrong. He knew Hadfield; he was as tricky as a wild bronc.

Dirk Jordan said, 'Sure, I'll do that Sam. We got that sheriff neatly tied up in a cave in the base o' that butte. We've got it planned, huh?'

He was fairly sure of his role but he knew he was taking risks. He had to time things; hand over the blasted sheriff and get to hell out before some cuss decided to throw lead. He had it figured out how to do it, though.

Bert Skinner was the fourth member of the outfit, and he figured he had a good job. He had to help keep the cattle herded together, look out for strays after the Double J men had gone to pick up the sheriff. Cows couldn't shoot at him, and Sam Hadfield had said they'd start driving the cattle into the hill country near Turtle Back soon as the Juana waddies had gone. It seemed that Hadfield had another couple of men hiding way back ready to ride in on the scene and earn some money.

'You see, my friends, when we drive the cattle nearer to Turtle Back, we are close to good companions who will start shooting if Lopez decides to take over the sheriff and then ride after his cattle. If he does that, he will hit rifle fire from fellows who do not love him.'

'Seems fair enough,' said Bert Skinner. 'Once we get the steers near Turtle Back we can hang on to them. As you say, we got itchy fingered gun hands back there who'll throw lead just for the hell of it.'

The four men sat their horses for some time and went over the facts of the set-up, each one agreeing with the others while holding on to secret thoughts. They were an unlovely bunch of bad-hats and had never been trusted by anyone, not even their mothers, for a long time.

They had their jobs outlined by Sam Hadfield, for about the fourth time, and it all seemed feasible. Cattle were as good as money in the bank because Hadfield had his buyers who would enter Turtle Back before the dust created by the herd had settled. There would be no fooling around. The cattle would vanish, disposed of to a number of unscrupulous outlets, within hours – and if Lopez had planned any trickery he would have his work cut out to retrieve that herd.

They waited, impatient horses pawing the earth. With every minute the mass of slow-moving cattle came nearer, bawling, raising dust, contained by the cowboys and vaqueros. In that huge flat of land, below the hill on which they stood, the cattle were a blackish,

119

swirling mass, their onward progression slow, but they were covering ground just the same.

Sam Hadfield judged it was time to send Mick out with his instructions to John Lopez.

'You know what to say. They have to leave the herd – now. All of them have to ride away – to the butte where they will pick up the sheriff. Dirk will be there to meet them. As soon as those cowhands have left, Bert and I will ride down to the herd and take over. As soon as the cattle get into the hill trails, I've got another two men to help out. You, Mick, will of course help out as soon as Lopez's men have gone.'

Sam Hadfield's rich voice boomed authoritatively, as if he had no doubt of success

Dirk Jordan had been staring at the distant riders who circled the oncoming herd. They were dark shapes in the bright sunlight that hid the dry land, but they were recognisable. Most men knew John Lopez, he was seen occasionally in Cactus Plain, on his way to the bank. There was another rider however who seemed to stick out to Dirk Jordan's sour gaze.

He could see the hunched figure of Rod Kane, taut in his saddle, the big black prancing close to John Lopez.

'See that, Bert – it's right – that blamed yarn we heard about the deputy. Damned if I can figure it out …'

Breathed Bert Skinner, 'How? How in blazes did he do it?'

There was no more time for conjecture, for Mick

kicked his cayuse forward at a signal from Sam
Hadfield, and Dirk knew it was time for him to ride
swiftly to the butte. He nudged the horse into a trot,
threw a backwards glance and saw Mick edging his
brown cayuse down the slope towards the bawling
herd and watching riders. He hoped everything would
go all right for the range-hand, not because he had
any regard for him – he could drop dead – but
because if one thing went wrong the whole blamed
thing could blow up. Mick had a few hundred yards to
cover to get within hailing distance of the Double J
men, but he, Dirk, would keep his distance – certainly
out of Colt range.

A drop into broken ground cut Dirk Jordan off
from the scene. He had to give attention to his route
and get the mustang moving. Hooves dug madly at
loose earth; he crouched low in the saddle, his hat
tugged firmly down, and his gun and holster snug on
his thigh.

As he cut across the country, leaving the sounds of
the big herd well behind, he thought again of the
troublesome deputy. The man was getting under his
hide. He hated his guts on account of many things.
The beating he had received rankled, and it wasn't
just that he had shot Clay Latimer dead; it was Rod
Kane's upright manner, his claim to a clear
conscience, and his standing among folks in Cactus
Plain. All this Dirk Jordan hated because he had none
of these things. He was a bum – and he knew it on the
odd occasions when he reflected on his life. He was a

lot older than the youthful deputy sheriff. He was a man without possessions or a job. No employer wanted him – unless he got day work hammering railroad ties, gut-slogging for pennies a day.

The deputy walked tall among law-abiding men: an object for a spiteful, murderous man to hate.

Well, the swine had escaped, but maybe there'd be another chance, another day.

Dirk Jordan reached the tall, towering red butte after some fast riding, his mustang blowing and lathered. He had given the animal no mercy. It stood still while he dismounted, a hardy, wiry horse quivering with exertion. He gave it no more thought, but led it to a stunted bush that grew out of the reddish soil at the base of the butte and hitched the leathers to the thorn branches. Then he walked stiffly, like a man just off a saddle, towards the black mouth of a cave.

His job now was to expect the Double J riders – and the deputy – because they would be told to ride to the butte but nothing else. They were not to be told that the sheriff was inside the cave. Dirk would inform them when they appeared – and then he would make sure he got out fast.

That was the way it was planned. Sam Hadfield expected the whole thing to work. Maybe Sam had other little plans – for his own personal safety – if anything went wrong.

Dirk Jordan dodged into the cold depths of the cave and stopped when he saw the gagged and bound figure of Sheriff Joe Clark.

'So you're still here.' He grinned. 'Nice o' you to stick around, Sheriff. You're a dollar bonanza ...'

Joe Clark's eyes glittered and he struggled futilely against his bonds. His hat was perched lop-sidedly on his head, revealing the red scar where the bullet had creased him. It was a nasty wound, thick with congealed blood. The elderly lawman was pale, unshaven, his grey moustache a ragged ornament. He looked ill.

'All right – you're still around,' sneered Dick Jordan. 'Just checkin'. After all, a mountain cat could ha' been in here an' made a meal outa you!' He went out of the cave, chuckling.

He stood for some moments, staring around at the terrain. The trail out for him was well-defined in his brain. He had settled on it for a fast getaway as soon as he could bawl to the expected riders where they could find the sheriff. He wanted to choose a high bit of ground which was handy for him, so that he could shout the few words that constituted his part of the bargain and then make a flying start to his getaway. He hardly cared whether the men picked up the sheriff or not, but the chore would keep them busy for a few minutes. It was part of the bargain Sam Hadfield had insisted they should carry out to avoid stirring up more grief.

Dirk Jordan found his vantage point and led his horse up the narrow furrow in the ground. He rolled a cigarette and settled down to wait. He figured it wouldn't be long. Pretty soon he'd ride like hell out of here, with dollars to pick up at the end of the trail.

The long, lean range-rider called Mick had warily ridden his horse down to the dusty perimeter of the herd and then checked the animal. The creature pranced at the sight of the steers; the bawling of cattle upset it. Mick held the horse in control and shouted his message, watching narrowly out of his slitted eyes for sign of any gun-happy galoot. But no one whipped out a sixgun. They stared from under wide-brimmed hats as if anxious, for the moment, to avoid trouble. Mick shouted, ready to dig in his rowels.

'You got to ride for the red butte – way over to the west. Everybody! That means the lot! Leave the herd. You'll meet a hombre near the butte – an' he'll tell yuh where to find the sheriff. Got that?'

'Can we trust you?' the demand came from John Lopez.

'That's the instructions!' the harsh shout hurled at them. 'I want no arguments! Everybody ride out. The sheriff will be found when yuh git to the butte …'

Mick inched his horse back, warily watching the men as they exchanged glances.

On the brow of the hill, just below the ridge, Sam Hadfield waited, the smooth jowls of the fat man's face now tight with caution.

John Lopez conferred with his ramrod and the deputy. 'We've got to play it safe until we find the sheriff … so that's the way they want it played … everybody

124

ride to the butte … well, let's go …'

With a wave to the men riding on the perimeter of the herd he set off across the semi-arid flat to the west. Rod Kane turned and waved to some of the waddies who were not sure what was expected of them. The men saw the signal and began to race to the west, horses outstretched.

Sam Hadfield watched them depart with some satisfaction, turning with a sneer on his fat face to the man near him.

'Well, that disposes of that little part of the drama, my friend. So far, so good, as the novelist Dickens would say – but then you haven't heard of him, have you, my ignorant companion?' He stared shrewdly down at the flat again, at the distant dots of the receding riders. 'Come. We've got about thirty minutes to get this herd moving again, segundo.'

Slowly, the two men picked a way down the slope to the now halted herd.

There was one thing the smart Sam Hadfield did not know. About four miles away to the east of the flat land, hiding under an overhanging shelf of rock and awaiting a signal, were a dozen US troopers under the command of a Lieutenant Gilbert.

Their movements had been made very carefully so that they had reached their point unobserved. So far as they knew, no wandering rider had seen them, so their presence should not be known to any man from Turtle Back.

Lieutenant Gilbert waited for the signal. He was

sure there was time yet to raise a merry war dance among the rustling ransomers, but it would have to be after the safety of the sheriff was ensured.

11

Worried Badmen

Rod Kane crouched low in the saddle, his mind on one big factor. He wanted to see Joe Clark alive and God help the hellions if he wasn't! Probably the outlaws had looked after the sheriff to the extent of making sure he lived – he was the key to the gift of a herd of beef. Any other trickery would earn them a retaliation that would be more than furious.

He knew about the troopers. John Lopez had got word at the last moment. It was a trump card which, if all went well, would show the outlaws just how much they had bitten off.

The big black pounded along with the others, a bunch of riders hell-bent on one thing – to get Sheriff Joe Clark to safety. Then anything could happen.

At that moment this was the only detail in Rod Kane's mind as he kept the black at full gallop. It was a sort of single track line of thought; they had to meet

127

a rider near the red butte, a well-known landmark in that region. The man would know the whereabouts of Joe Clark.

It was perhaps a shaky sort of arrangement that the thieves had dreamed up, one that could go wrong if someone got trigger-happy, but at the moment they had to go along with it.

The red butte was visible for miles, rising out of the huge plain. It was a solitary finger near the base of some hills that rambled back to Turtle Back some miles away and rose like some volcanic eruption from the bed of the plain, eroded by time and winter rains and scouring sand. High above the foothills, it was a red rock monument from the dawn of time.

Joe Clark must be somewhere near the red butte, but only the man they had to meet knew where.

The rapid tattoo of hooves beat at the dry earth, sending up echoes along the silent plain that told the waiting man of their approach. To him the noise made by the group of riders was like an angry roll of drums.

The bunch of horses and riders surged up to the base of the butte and circled, still at high speed, and then whirled the animals around and halted in a swirl of dust. Horses snorted and quivered and jerked heads. The men threw searching glances all around.

Dirk Jordan chose this moment to thrust his head over the ridge of shale and tufted grasses that had hidden him. As his movement was observed, he shouted:

'Look in the cave! That's all, gents! No tricky business! I got hot slugs for the first feller who follows me!'

It was a desperate threat and he knew it as he hurtled on to the saddle of his waiting horse and rowelled it out of the big cleft. The horse sprang into urgent movement, spurred viciously by its rider, and headed down to the goat-like track through the foothills.

In that second of swift reaction from the bunch of men, Rod Kane decided on one thing. He had noted the identity of Dirk Jordan and that was all he needed to motivate his next few seconds of action.

He knew now that the sheriff would be found and that there were plenty to take care of him. That was all that mattered. Now he wanted to get Dirk Jordan.

Rod's big black sprang like an arrow after the hellion. Hooves dug savagely into loose soil. The horse climbed in a series of lithe leaps and reached the thin trail that snaked through the rounded slopes of the foothills. The track wasn't recognisable as such. It was merely a barely definable way through the limitless sprawl of slopes that seemed to go on for ever. His horse got into a fine stride, man and beast both taking chances of a tumble.

Dirk Jordan was still in sight. His mustang, wiry though it was, seemed to be a bit tired. Maybe the man had thrashed it on the ride over to the butte. Anyway, smaller than the black, it was not making any better speed along this winding, treacherous track.

Rod Kane let the man know he was after him – as if there was any doubt. He had seen Dirk Jordan throw backward glances. Rod aimed three swift shots at the bucking, swerving rider, knowing there was only a lucky chance of a hit. Grimly, he holstered the gun again, knowing there was not time to reload and he would have to save those last three slugs.

He was determined that this man would not escape to plan other vicious crimes. He hated to think Dirk Jordan would escape – and he might, because he was clear of the bunch handling the herd. Rod Kane was determined to ride the man down to the ground.

The chase went on for a mile – and another mile – heading towards the outlaw town, where desperate men were all too ready to lend a hand against the law.

The lucky break came for Rod Kane a moment later when the mustang stumbled and fell on a badly holed stretch of ground. The small horse rolled over, throwing Dirk Jordan heavily to one side. The animal screamed and threshed with its legs and eventually pushed itself up and hobbled away. Dirk Jordan had not wasted a tenth of a second. Jarred as he must have been by the fall, he nevertheless slithered immediately behind a scattering of round boulders and snapped off a shot at Rod Kane.

The deputy whipped his horse around with equally fast reactions. Hooves dug and sent chips of rock and soil spurting in many directions. The animal sprang gamely, haunches rippling, head outstretched. In a second or two they reached the shelter of a fold in the ground, a smooth hump of soil and prickly bushes. As the black quivered to a halt, safe from a bullet, Rod jumped to the ground and hefted his gun into his hand. He held tight on to the leathers, cast fast looks around him, sizing up the lay of the land.

One thing was sure – Dirk Jordan was grounded, therefore his escape had failed. What was going on back at the butte Rod did not know. He sure hoped that the sheriff had been found, that the signal would be sent to the waiting troopers, that the other outlaws would get a taste of punishment, and that the herd would be retrieved.

But right now he had Dirk Jordan flattened behind those skeleton-white boulders. The man would come out with his hands up, or die.

Rod found a big stone and wrapped it around the reins and so ground-hitched his mount. He hugged the yellow soil underneath him, crawled up to the ridge of the fold. He got a glimpse of the sun-bleached boulders and snapped off his three shots at the hellion. Then, quickly, he reloaded. There was silence from the other man. It seemed he was waiting for a glimpse of his enemy, or thinking out a means of escape from his predicament.

Rod knew this was a situation that could waste a man's time, pin him down indefinitely to an almost useless exchange of gunshots.

Grimly, he decided that was no good. He wanted this over and done with. There were many other chores he had to do.

He yelled: 'Jordan – throw your gun away an' come out! I'm goin' to get you …'

Two shots spat out and the slugs bit dust off the ridge of yellow soil. It wasn't bad shooting and warned Rod that he had to keep his head down.

'D'you want to live, Jordan? Come on out an' give it up! After all, you haven't killed anyone yet. I'm very much alive – as you can see! Give up – an' all you'll face is a spell in the hoosegow for kidnap—'

'Go to hell, Deputy!' came the bellow. 'I'll kill you!'

Rod Kane wasted no more time. He thought he saw a way around the other man. A move like this would keep him guessing and might get the drop on him. Slithering along the bottom of the fold, cursing mildly at the prickly thicket, he began a circling movement. The land was a series of humps, as if some burrowing creature had thrown up mounds. He crawled patiently on, circling, gaining some height. Then, from a vantage point, he chanced a swift glance at the direction of the white boulders.

He saw movement a long way past the rocks. He wasn't surprised to note that while he had been crawling, the other man had been trying to find another position among some bigger rocks.

Rod Kane took a deep breath – and then sprang. He had decided on a hell-for-leather attack that had to succeed.

He ran forward, leaping, jumping, swerving like a crazy galoot. He knew he would draw Dirk Jordan out to fire at such an open target, but he'd be on the move, ready to shoot back.

At the same time, his fast rush brought him right

132

around the other man and he had the satisfaction of seeing the outlaw scrambling desperately to another hiding place. A swift crouching leap, and the man fired at the running deputy. The bullet whistled its warning song as it tore past Rod's head.

Then his own gun was bucking in his hand, spitting defiant lead at the shape that tried to hug the ground even closer. Rod Kane sprang again, just as another slug tore thin air. At the end of a succeeding leap he swivelled and crouched and triggered fast as lighting. The Colt barked and he kept on moving. He jumped with a crash behind some scattered rocks and poked his gun out.

Then he heard the groan and the cursing voice of the badman. 'Damn yuh, Kane! Damn you to hell.'

The grim-faced deputy slowly peered over the intervening ground, at the writhing man now completely out of cover. He was rolling slowly backwards and forwards in pain, holding a hand to his chest.

Rod got carefully to his feet, gun poking forward in a tight hand. He stared at Dirk Jordan and walked two or three feet forward.

'Are you hurt? Ready to pack it in?'

'Looks like it, don't it …?'

Some sixth sense warned Rod Kane at the last possible moment and he threw himself sideways as the other man's gun whipped up in a hand that was far from belonging to a dying man. Dirk Jordan's gun exploded – but the slug hit empty air inches from the deputy.

Simultaneously, Rod's weapon spat its last dreadful reply.

The bullet hit Dirk Jordan between the eyes. The head rammed back and as Rod Kane bounded forward the man was already a corpse.

He stared down at the bearded, thick-set body for a long time, watching the blood bubble through the ghastly hole in the head. The tense, keyed-up condition of every nerve in Rod's body gradually faded and left him feeling cold and in-drawn. The man he'd killed spilled his blood on to the dry soil, a vivid red mixing with the yellow. Now that there was no enemy to fight, Rod Kane felt sickness rise in his throat. He did not want to kill. Revenge always seemed sweet against a living, tormenting enemy – but when that individual became a shattered corpse there was no satisfaction, just an inward grimness that hit zero.

However, there was always work to do, like the little chores of clearing up after death. He went in search of the man's mustang and found it. The animal had corralled itself between some rocks. Rod led it back and hoisted the dead man to the saddle, crosswise, like a sack of corn. He tied the body securely with the rope that had been looped around the saddle-horn, and then he went in the direction of his own black, leading the mustang.

In this way, Rod Kane rode back to the red butte, once again bringing a dead man back on his own cayuse. It was better this way, for he was a lawman and even the enemy was entitled to burial and witnesses to

134

note the way he had died.

He found John Lopez and the sheriff and a Mexican vaquero still at the butte. The other riders had hit the trail, heading back to the position of the herd, ready to take over after the troopers had dealt with the Turtle Back hardcases.

'So you got your man,' commented John Lopez, looking up as Rod Kane rode down to the flat land.

'He's one dead hombre,' returned the deputy. 'And I'm gettin' over the feeling of remorse at killing him. This man tried to …'

'So that is the man?' The rancher turned again to Joe Clark who was sitting on the ground, his back against a small rock.

Rod slid off his horse, went swiftly to the sheriff. Joe Clark looked up weakly and tried to grin.

'How the blazes are you, you old buzzard?' Rod asked cheerfully. 'Why in heck ain't you on a horse?'

'Because I'm not as tough as a buzzard,' was the attempt at repartee. 'But I'll make it. They've left a nag for me …' It was true, there was a horse standing by.

'You will be ready to ride, my friend, as soon as you find the use of your legs,' said John Lopez encouragingly. 'You are a bit weak with loss of blood. Your legs have been bound too long…'

'All right – let's have another go at standin',' grunted Joe Clark, and with Rod's help he got up and stood stiffly on his feet. 'Heck, I'm all right!' He glanced at the deputy. 'How is Muriel? How'd she take it?'

'She'll be better when you arrive back home,' said Rod with a grin.

Rod Kane helped him mount the spare horse. Joe Clark slowly took up the leathers, found the stirrups. He pulled his hat squarely on to his head, covering the nasty scar. He smiled again. 'I feel better. Let's go.'

'You are welcome to stay at the Juana Ranch,' began John Lopez as he sat his fine palomino. 'You are always welcome, my friend … we can talk about many things …'

Joe Clark straightened his grey moustache and squared his shoulders. '*Amigo*, I want to see my wife – but let me thank you for everythin'. Not many men would offer to pay kidnappers the price they demanded of you. A man like me doesn't have many friends – bein' on the right side o' the law is a lonely business – and you, John, are the best I've got …'

'Do you forget your young deputy, Joe?' smiled the rancher. 'He has worked hard and men have tried to kill him!'

'He'll be wearin' my badge some day!' grunted Joe Clark. 'We'd better move – afore I fall off this nag!'

They rode slowly at first, away from the red butte that rose from the plain, leaving the place that had probably seen many strange events in its ancient history, and made a steady progress eastward. A silence fell on the men at first, seeming to match the fall of the sun to the western horizon. The day was wearing on and, with some tensions gone, Rod Kane felt the pangs of hunger.

136

His last meal had been a long way back, before they had started to drive the herd, at the Juana Ranch. He lit a cigarette and offered the makings to the Mexican vaquero. Rod did not smoke often and then only to pass the time. He then rolled a smoke for Joe Clark. John Lopez declined the other with a smile. A sulphur match was struck and the light passed around.

One of the Juana Ranch outfit came riding over at great speed, a black patch at first, that gradually became larger as his horse covered the vast flat at racing speed. The man reined in beside them, his horse swishing a lively tail.

'The troopers have gone after them hellions,' he informed them, 'and the hands have got the herd under way, Mr Lopez.'

'That's great news, Luke! How about those outlaws? Did the troopers haul any in?'

'The sidewinders made off like they was scared to hell, Mr Lopez! I was busy with the beef, but I figure the troopers rode hard at 'em – maybe into Turtle Back.'

'We'll get all the news soon enough,' said John Lopez. 'The main thing is my friend here is safe and sound – as you can see.'

'Looks like you've put it over on them rogues,' grunted Sheriff Joe Clark.

The news cheered up the little party. Joe Clark seemed to ride better in his saddle, as if feeling stronger. The men lost their silence and began to talk, putting each other in the picture, giving the details of what had happened, how they had made out in their own way. Rod Kane told the sheriff everything – how Long Haired Jim North had helped him, practically saving his life. He told Joe Clark about the men working the canyon for sign of the lost mine shaft that was reputed to hide the age-old treasure of the padres. He mentioned how he had seen Al Smith out there and how he had checked on the man's identity.

And he mentioned how Jim North was still looking for the mysterious Gideon James.

12

Unlawful
Search

A day later Joe Clark had been restored to a wife who cared, and who was wonderfully glad to see him, Rod Kane sought out Long Haired Jim at the barn where he was still sleeping with his grey stallion. If anything, the drifter looked even more grubby, his new blue-checked shirt stained already with what looked like a mixture of egg and beer.

Only his gunbelt, snug around the top of his leather trousers, was clean – and the pearl-butted gun that was holstered there. Dirty or not, Jim North was glad to see the deputy.

'Hi! You're lookin' fine.'

'I feel better,' said Rod. 'And the sheriff is pickin' up fine too. I wonder if you'd do somethin' for me?'

'Sure. What is it?'

'Al Smith has a room on the second floor of The Imperial. I know exactly where it is ...'

'You still got bugs about that gent?'

'Maybe. Now listen. Al Smith has left town – I've just seen him ride out an' I figure he's gone to that canyon way out by the Shadow Mountains …'

'So?'

'I want to look into his room,' said Rod slowly.

'Hey, is that legal?' Jim North got up from the straw on which he was lying.

'I'm not too darned concerned about what is legal and what is not at the moment – where that hombre is concerned,' snapped Rod Kane.

'You don't like him,' remarked Jim North shrewdly.

Rod's face became red and taut. 'All right, Jim – so I don' like the man!'

'You got that gal in mind,' pursued the drifter. 'Waal, she's a mighty pretty filly …'

'You've seen her?'

'Yeah – saw her in that dress shop.' Long Haired Jim whistled. 'It was too bad you had to plug her brother.'

Rod walked around the barn. 'All right, Jim – I admit I'm wearin' a chip where Al Smith is concerned. I went along to see June late last night and – and –' He halted.

Jim North's eyes searched his face. 'Waal, go on! What she do – throw yuh out?'

'Al Smith was there … damn-well drinking coffee and – and – talkin' real smooth!'

'And she with no chaperone!' ejaculated Jim North.

'Oh, June Latimer is a real up-to-date gal!' flared Rod. 'You should hear her talk some time! She's got some rebel ideas – thinks a woman is equal to a man—'

'Now that's durned crazy …'

'Well, it don't make much sense – but I – I respect her opinions. She really is a wonderful gal! Anyway, she let me in last night and I tried to git a word in – but I guess she was playin' me off against that blamed Al Smith. Women are darned hard to understand sometimes, Jim.'

'Me – I'd sooner yap to my hoss!' said Jim.

Rod Kane bunched one fist into the palm of his hand. 'Al Smith doesn't know that I saw him in the canyon. I took good care not to mention that. Only you an' the sheriff, and John Lopez know about it, and they won't blab.'

'Some joker cut you down,' Long Haired Jim pointed out. 'An' when you came round, you was in a wagon – like you told me.'

'Al Smith doesn't know that. He was real smooth last night, complimenting me on the way the outlaws had been handled. But playin' me down all the time. I know what his game is up at the canyon, but I'm not so sure what he's up to with June. I don't want her to get hurt …'

'You mean she might take a fancy to this cuss?' said Jim North roughly.

'She's free to do what she likes,' snapped Rod. 'But I don't trust Al Smith …'

'You can say that again!'

'All right – maybe it's June – maybe I don't think so straight where she's concerned.'

'Women git a galoot like that sometimes,' observed Jim North.

141

'I admit that Al Smith has me riled – although the man did help me once when I tangled with Dirk Jordan and his pal. I want to get him out of my mind, once and for all. I've checked on him by means of that telegram – sure. Now I figure to look in his room.'

'What' the heck for?'

'Papers – anything – identification – a letter maybe…'

'But the telegram checks. He's from Cimarron …'

Rod nodded. 'Yeah, that checks …'

'You figger to find more?'

'That's about the size of it, Jim. Now will you help me?'

'Sure,' said Jim promptly. 'Anythin', pardner. You an' me – we get along. What d'you want me to do?'

'Nothing much. We go into The Imperial and when no one is looking we walk up to the second floor. I'll go into his room an' you can keep a lookout.'

'You know his room?'

'I know it.'

'An' maybe you got a key, huh?'

'It so happens, Jim, I've been in The Imperial before on the manager's instructions, when he had a cold-blooded murder on his hands, an' I know the type of key. We've got the same series in the sheriff's office.'

'You could look around without me …'

'Maybe, but a lookout saves a mite of discomfort sometimes.'

In truth it was a silent Rod Kane who walked into The Imperial with Jim North. They stood at the bar for some moments, knocking back two whiskies for which Rod paid. Then, with a wary expression in bleak eyes, Rod led the way up the stairs when the bartender was busy. As to the few patrons, they were unconcerned about the movements of others at this early time of the day. So Rod and his helper came to the door numbered seven. A twist of the small key, and the brown-painted door swung in.

'You stick around the passage,' said Rod. 'If anybody comes along – the manager – cleaner – just start talkin' loudly and I'll hear you.'

'I'll talk loudly, sure thing – tryin' to explain jest what I'm a-doin' up here ...'

'Well, we won't see Al Smith. I'm tolerably sure he's headed for the Shadow Mountains.'

With those parting words, Rod slid into the room and quietly closed the door behind him.

He knew with some grim certainty that he was fooling around behind a man's back, and it wasn't a feeling he enjoyed. He'd have admitted instantly that he doubted his own judgement of Al Smith. Maybe he was just plumb annoyed because the man had got on the inside track with June. True enough, the cool, confident man was playing an illegal game up in the Shadow Mountains, prospecting around on territory where he had no right. He was doing it secretly, which proved he had no authorisation.

Altogether however, Rod Kane was not happy about this intrusion into Al Smith's affairs but seeing he was now on the spot, he would get on with it.

143

The first step was to examine a chest of drawers. They were not locked and so he eased them out, one at a time, and looked through the contents. The top one contained items of clothing, two fancy shirts, two pairs of thick grey socks and a new red necktie. Rod looked into another drawer. It was half-empty, holding only a box of rifle cartridges and another of Colt .45 ammunition. Rod stared at the supplier's name printed on the boxes – a firm named Brown, Caliente, Nevada.

Nevada! That was a heck of a long way from Cimarron, Texas. What did it mean, if anything?

It meant the durned ammunition had come from Caliente, Nevada and nothing much else. It did not prove anything. Maybe Al Smith had once visited the place.

He looked into another drawer, the largest one. He immediately found himself looking at a carpetbag, something he did not associate with the suave Al Smith. Somehow he thought of the man as a horse-man, complete with saddlebags. The carpetbag seemed something a drummer might carry – a man who travelled the railroad or stage.

Rod opened it with an expressionless face. He hardly knew what to expect, although he knew it was almost empty, for it was lying flat in the drawer. He saw the small bundle of papers at once. Taking them out, he began to peruse them.

They were mainly letters addressed to Al Smith, El Bar B Ranch, Cimarron, Texas. They were business letters and the subject matter was mostly cattle and of no real importance.

Rod put them back, a dismal feeling of futile prying overwhelming him. He was a fool. So Al Smith was just what he claimed – a rancher.

He flipped through the letters and bills, almost ready to thrust them back into the carpetbag when he noticed the 5 x 3 sepia photograph. It showed a man and a woman posing proudly for the rare event. The man was tall, handsome with a fine moustache and he was blond haired. He wore a good dark suit, a white shirt and black string tie. The woman was dressed in a tight-fitting gown and very wasp-waisted, as was the fashion.

On the back of the photograph, in a fine copperplate, was the short caption: '*Al and Mary Smith, Cimarron, 1890.*'

Rod Kane stared, seeing in detail the definite outline of the man's fine face. This was Al Smith, rancher!

His brain was not fooling him; he was thinking as clearly as a good mirror reflects the truth.

The man in the photograph was Al Smith – he knew it! And that was all he wanted – for the Al Smith who carried a Frontier Colt and searched for hidden treasure in the Shadow Mountains was a fake!

Whatever his name or his identity, he was not the same man on this photograph. There were little differences in the cut of the jaw, the shape of the nose, the details that distinguish one man from another although they may even be brothers. True, both men were blond, fair, and wore thin moustaches and had much the same build.

But Al Smith, the gun-toter, was not the man in the photograph.

Rod Kane slipped the sepia print inside his shirt, buttoned it up again, and all at once he felt better. Gone were the nagging doubts. Confidence in his inner hunch surged back and gave him new authority.

He was going to the door when he heard Long Haired Jim's voice raised in loud tones.

'Say, d'you hang out in this hotel, pardner?'

Another man's voice returned a sharp comment. Then: 'Say, I'm kinda lost, pal. Can you tell me if there's a galoot name o' Jones a-stayin' in this place?'

Rod Kane guessed at once that Jim North was playing tag with some man outside, his loud voice a warning.

Rod waited, expecting the new arrival to enter some room or otherwise go about his business.

But a key grated in the lock and a moment later a man opened the door – and walked straight into Rod Kane's firmly-held gun.

The man, bulky, thirtyish, clad in a jerkin and dusty trousers, stared open-mouthed at the deputy.

'You! What …?'

Long Haired Jim was pretty prompt. He sidled in behind the man and closed the door so that anybody passing would not feel obliged to interfere.

'Have I seen you somewhere before?' Rod demanded, staring.

146

The man hesitated. 'You're the deputy ...'

'Sure – you can see that. Who are you?'

'What in hell are you doin' in here?' returned the man.

'You tell me why you've come to this room?' snapped Rod Kane.

'Mr Smith sent me. I got a key. I've got a right to open this door.'

'What does Mr Smith want?'

'I met him out on the trail. He wanted me to fetch some gear ...'

'What's your name?' asked Rod. The gun did not waver.

The bulky man hesitated and then said: 'I'm Dan Bale. I work for Mr Smith. Deputy or not, you've no right to be in this room.'

'I've got a feeling I've seen you somewhere,' pursued Rod. 'Now what the heck is jigging around at the back of my mind?'

'You've no right ...' began Dan Bale again.

'You're the man at the camp in the canyon!' flashed the deputy. 'The one that took a look in the wagon an' then slapped off my horse!'

Dan Bale shifted uneasily. 'Now look here, Deputy, I'm a peaceful man an' I don't want trouble. I've done nothin' wrong ...'

'You and that boss of yours are exploring territory forbidden to white men unless you got special authority from the Bureau for Indian Affairs – an' you and Al Smith just haven't got that permit!' rapped the deputy.

147

'That ain't a crime.'

'You'll find out different if the troopers come to move you on.'

'Hell, you seem to know a lot!'

'Al Smith's little secret venture won't be a secret much longer – apart from anything else.' Rod was thinking about the man's fake identity.

'Hell, don't you know who I am?' ground out the man. 'I'm the man who saved your blasted life, Mister Deputy! Maybe I should have let you swing!'

Rod Kane stared, his knuckles around the gun butt going white. 'You're the feller who cut me down?'

'You're blamed right I did! You was dangling when me an' Wally drove up in the wagon – an' you was about dead!'

'Go on.'

'I jest cut you down. Well, we didn't know what to do – an' we saw you was a deputy sheriff. So we bundled you into the wagon …'

'You maybe saved my life,' said Rod slowly. He stared at the man with a mixture of curiosity and doubt. The gun seemed suddenly stupid. He lowered it. In any case the man did not pack a weapon. Rod looked again, still feeling sore from the painful treatment he'd received.

'Look, all I want is some gear for Mr Smith,' began Dan Bale again.

'Your boss ain't Smith!' snapped Rod harshly. 'That ain't his real name. He's got questions to answer – and

I aim to ask them. I've got some new hunches about Al Smith.'

'Ain't Smith?' repeated the man. 'Waal, now, a lot of men change their names ...'

Long Haired Jim's shrewd, range-wise eyes were staring at Rod's grim face, guessing there was something new.

'The best thing you can do is ride out o' town,' began Rod, looking at the other man. 'Just ride on, friend. Because that little venture in the Shadow Mountains is due to blow sky-high.'

'What the hell are yuh gettin' at?'

'I'd like to help you,' said Rod quietly. 'I'm not forgettin' you saved my life or at least from a worse roastin'. There ain't much I can do for you except offer advice. Ride out. That treasure won't be found ...'

'Smith has a map!' Anger began to well up in Dan Bale. For so long he had clung to the notion that there were riches due to come his way – and now this deputy was blowing the idea sky-high. It was enough to rile any man. 'The boss got a map from an old Indian that was dyin'. This map had been drawn by his father – an' maybe on instructions from his father! I tell you, it's jest a matter o' time afore we find that stuff.'

Rod shook his head. 'Listen, Dan Bale. I know your outfit is workin' illegally. I've just got to send messages to the Indian Agent an' the troopers would be there the next day clearing you off what is Indian Territory.'

Dan Bale's mouth twisted. 'Tarnation, Deputy – we got a fortune waitin' us somewhere – in those hills –

149

that canyon. We'll find it – wind an' rain has scoured the rock faces – but we'll find it! The shaft was filled with clay and rubble – we'll know it when we see it! Why don't yuh give us a chance? I gave you one! You're lucky to be alive!'

'I appreciate it. I can understand, Dan Bale, that it's a mighty bitter pill to swallow – but I'll say it again. The venture is all washed up.' He made a half-turn. 'I'm ridin' out to that canyon right away.'

It was in that second, when Rod's attention was off the man that Dan Bale darted for the door. For someone so bulky he was pretty fast when he acted, and he had wrenched the door open and leaped into the passage before either Rod or Jim North could stop him.

'Let him go,' said Rod. It was an instant decision, a moment of weakness which was to have repercussions.

'He'll ride out and warn Smith!'

'I think he'll take good advice and just move on,' said Rod.

It was a mistaken opinion, as he was to discover...

'What's all this about Smith not bein' that galoot's real name?' Long Haired Jim was a surprisingly fast man on the uptake. 'You've found somethin', pardner?'

Rod silently showed the man the sepia print. 'Tell me what you think about this.' He waited.

Inside a few significant moments Jim North gave his answer. 'This ain't Al Smith – I mean the Al Smith we know ain't' the galoot in this picture!'

'Thanks for checking.' Rod took the photograph again. 'All right – I'm ridin' out. I want to know how come our Al Smith – or whatever his name is – got possession of these letters and photograph.'

'Yep – me too!' Long Haired Jim pulled his battered hat down on one side, a speculative gleam in his eyes.

'You?'

'I'm in on this, *amigo* – an' don't try to horn me out.'

In that mood there was nothing Rod Kane could do to stop the thin drifter from getting his horse from the barn and accompanying him on the ride out.

Rod Kane halted only long enough to inform Sheriff Joe Clark that he and Jim North were taking the long ride out to the Shadow Mountains. The sheriff looked up from his office chair.

'If you've got something on that feller – go ahead. I'm not stopping you. But watch it! Remember, a lawman needs evidence.'

Rod was still smiling at Joe Clark's fatherly advice when he and Long Haired Jim rode at a fast clip out of Cactus Plain. The morning sun was warming the land again, with seemingly little prospect of rain, and the grass was turning yellow. They cut away from the main trail, climbing ridges and going helter-skelter into the valley below. Rod was saddle-tuned to the black's every move, knowing when to push the beast and when to ease up. The journey was not one that could be rushed. They could see the faint blue tinge of the mountain range in the distance, when they climbed a ridge.

151

'That gal ain't a-goin' to like seein' that picture,' Long Haired Jim observed during one of the easy riding spells. 'For a start, our Al Smith ain't the galoot in the picture – an' if he was, he's got a wife!'

'I follow your mixed reasoning,' said Rod, 'but don't worry – I'm not toadying to a girl. Our treasure-seeking friend will do the explainin'.'

'You always did figure him for a mystery man.'

'And I was right.'

'How'd he git those letters – an' the photograph?'

'We'll learn the truth – pretty soon,' was Rod's grim retort.

Long Haired Jim rode in silence for a long time, his jaws working on a chaw of baccy. Finally he emitted a stream of disgusting juice from his mouth, aiming to his right, away from Rod, and was then able to speak. His few words were surprising.

'You figure this galoot is Gideon James?'

'I wouldn't know.'

'Huh. Gideon James is dark-haired an' bearded.'

'Beards can be shaven.'

'Waal, now, that's a plumb accurate statement. And hows-about dark hair?'

Rod turned, unsmiling. 'Don't you know hair can be dyed?'

'Dyed? You don't say!'

'Even you, Jim – with hair as black as an Injun – could be made as fair as a blue-eyed little gal. Now you think about that, *amigo*!'

The horses headed fast towards a clump of tall

Washington palms, those desert trees common to the Arizona-California borderlands.

The man known as Dan Bale reached the canyon before the lawman and the drifter. He had had just that much head start, while Rod had been talking to the sheriff and getting horses prepared, and he got to the camp, in actual fact, shortly after Al Smith had tethered his horse.

He had followed his boss across the terrain, occasionally spotting his progress in the distance. He had not been within hailing distance, and, gunless, could not attract his attention. Anyway only time was involved before he was able to speak to Al Smith face to face.

The yellow walls of the canyon enclosed them like a box and held a silence that was age-old, broken only by the sounds the men made in the camp. Boots trudged against loose gravel and shale; horses nosed for the odd tufts of browned grass. Cholla cactus was everywhere, the first pink flowers showing. And all around, the bare rocks reflected the heat like an oven. It was hot out here. Coolness might be found only higher in the hills where the trees grew.

Dan Bale's shout made Al Smith turn. He was a lithe, smart figure in a spotless shirt, clean brown trousers unstained by sweat. His Frontier Colt lay snug in a thonged-down holster, his boots jingled with bright Mexican-style spurs. His hat shaded his lean, smiling face but oddly, it could be noted that his blue eyes were wary pools even in the simple reaction of turning with a smile to Dan Bale.

'Boss – there's trouble!'

'Yes?' Al Smith just waited, his smile only a shade fainter. 'What's the matter, Dan? Didn't you bring that chart I'd made?'

'I got stopped. That deputy was in your room at the hotel—'

Al Smith walked forward, arms dangling, hands lowering instinctively about his gunbelt. 'In my room! What did he say?'

'He pulled a gun on me … he said your name wasn't Smith.'

'Is that so? What else?'

Dan Bale stammered. 'Weren't much … he told me to git out of town. Said he was ridin' out here – *pronto*!'

'How the hell did he know this place?'

'I – I – don't know. He just knows about it.' Dan Bale's eyes flickered as his brain registered danger to himself. He saw old Wally Hands eyeing him, his mouth a bit slack, caution printed on his features.

'He just knew we're out here!' repeated Al Smith. 'Damned if I know how – but never mind. He's riding this way, huh?'

'Sure, sure, but you can deal with him, boss!' Dan Bale's eyes fell to the Frontier Colt.

'I can deal with him all right.'

'I reckon he'll bring a pardner with him.'

'Who?'

154

'Why – there was a black-haired feller with him – long haired – like an Injun.'

'Oh – indeed! I think I know the man.' There was a cool edge to his voice. 'Well, leave them to me.'

The other two men had edged up behind Wally Hands and had listened in silence to their boss's remarks. Then they exchanged doubtful glances; glanced around uncertainly as if troubled in mind. One man beat dust out of his clothes and then grated: 'Hell – I figured we were near to findin' that old mine shaft!'

'We'll find it,' snapped Al Smith. 'Just leave this interfering swine to me.'

'You aim to cut him down?'

'It seems we have no alternative – except ride out. But I tell you, men, we've marked out three likely places in this canyon. The snag is that the contour of the rock faces has been altered with the years. We've got to dig in a number of places – take samples of the soil – find a part of the rock wall that shows sign of being a filler.'

'This is gonna take time,' rasped one man. 'Durn it – I might ha' known we'd run out of luck!'

'Maybe there ain't no treasure,' said Wally Hands in disgust. 'You can't trust some of these old yarns – an' even a map – drawn by an Injun – you can't go by that!'

'Quit worryin'!' snapped Al Smith. 'I'll take care of everything. We'll have a few more days … and maybe we'll strike it rich. Once we find that old shaft, we'll get the treasure out mighty fast.'

'You'd gun 'em down?' queried Dan Bale.

'It's the only way. You want to be rich, don't you?' There was a sneer in Al Smith's cool tones.

'That jasper is a deputy. If he don't show up, the sheriff'll be out lookin' for him. What then? We can't shoot 'em all!'

'Just a few more days is all we want.'

'I'm a-goin',' muttered Dan Bale. 'This is sure played out. Gosh-darn it – all the flamin' work I've done out here. Treasure! Why, we're fools. That damned loot has been somewhere in these rocks for a hundred years – an' we ain't the first to try for it. Maybe it'll never be found. I'm ridin' out – while there's still time. I want no part of killin'.'

Al Smith's hand dropped to his gun – but he did not draw. A gunfighter by trade, he did not waste bullets or invite useless strife.

'All right, Dan – you go,' he said.

'I'm ridin' with my pardner,' muttered old Wally Hands. 'He's right. We can't stick around here any longer. Figure it out. If that deputy don't show up, the sheriff will be out scourin' the whole territory – an' he might call in the troopers. This is Injun country ...'

The two men walked away, trudging grimly across the shale towards the tents where they had some personal bits of gear such as grub-bags, water canteens. The other two men who had spent a few nights in the tents withdrew and began to talk in growling tones, obviously absolutely sick of the whole fruitless business.

One walked back to Al Smith. 'We're goin'. We're

156

ridin' out. Foolin' around on Injun territory is one thing – shootin' two men is another. We ain't gunfighters.'

'You're walking out on a fortune!' sneered Al Smith. 'The treasure is here – I know it.'

'Then you'd best dig for it,' said one man. 'Me – I'm goin'. Just one thing – don't dig yourself a grave!'

'You plumb fools!' Al Smith was angry now, a deadly cool anger that was all the worse for being controlled. 'Go ahead – ride out! Look after your rotten hides! Play it safe – your brainless kind always do! I'll dig a grave all right – but it'll be for that damned deputy – and that long-haired skunk. Then, some day I'll be back – with a new crew – and I'll find this treasure. I'll find it – if it takes years!'

Suddenly, the useless talk faded away as the four men fixed up their horses for the ride out. They wasted no more time. They acted like men who had suddenly made big decisions and they were through with words. Sullenly, one by one, they rode out of the canyon, past the sprawl of loose rock that marked the mouth. The sound of their horses' hoof-beats picked up into a rapid canter as they rode away. They were gone, to new scenes, another frontier town, or other plans that promised a living in a hard land.

Al Smith did not waste further time in anger. He knew his gun would have to speak for him because he wasn't riding away from danger – not yet. His gun would talk because that was the sort of action he understood. If he killed, he could ride out. He had done it before. He had notched up more kills than any two gunmen put

157

together – and there'd be more. Shoot and ride out. That had been his method for a long time.

When he had met up with that damned-fool lone rider, Al Smith, the encounter had ended when they'd quarrelled over a game of cards, right out there on the lonely land, just the two of them.

He had killed the man, of course. He was too slow with his sixgun. Then the idea of taking his identity had entered his mind. It had been easy. The man was his build and general appearance, except for the beard and hair. A barber in a small town had fixed that for him. The beard came off. His hair had been bleached.

He had started to call himself 'Al Smith' and in this manner entered Cactus Plain, the plan to search for the lost treasure in mind. He had had that map a long time. It was a venture he'd wanted to start for many a year. Now, with a new identity, he had figured he had the opportunity.

Al Smith waited for the two riders to show up.

He smiled thinly, recalling how he'd taken the gold from the black-haired drifter and how he'd dropped his much-notched pearl-butted gun. So the fool had kept it! Not only that, he had the audacity to search the trails for – Gideon James!

Well, that was a laugh because pretty soon the drifter would find him.

The gold had not lasted long. Gambling, good living, women – the list was easily compiled. He'd got a taste for big money, though – and that was why he'd wanted to find the lost treasure so badly.

158

He saw the two black dots a long way off from his position on a rocky promontory.

The deputy and the drifter. Some pair!

He could take care of them easily. He had lost none of his skill at gunmanship, even though he had lost his pearl-handled Colt. He'd bury them, ride out and return some day to find the lost treasure.

He did not bother to hide. He knew he was fast with a gun. If they wanted him, they'd have to draw – and they'd die. That would be the end of the interfering fools.

Rod Kane rode up and dismounted. He halted and was joined by Jim North. They spread out, walked forward, away from the horses. They stared up at the lone man.

'I think you're Gideon James – a wanted outlaw,' said Rod Kane quietly. 'You're wanted for murder.'

'Just one murder?' mocked the man.

'You dirty thievin' skunk!' yelled Jim North. 'You done took my gold!'

'It didn't last long,' said Gideon James. 'And you wouldn't know what to do with it – saddlebum!'

'You can come into town quietly,' said Rod Kane, 'or make a play …'

For a tense moment there was silence.

Then Gideon James laughed.

'I can kill both of you!' he sneered and, with blazing speed his gun leaped from the holster and fired.

A crazy pattern of mixed shots cracked the silent air. Three guns fired within a second. Slugs with

159

Instant Death written on them ripped the air. The slugs of one man, however, were a fraction faster. The pearl-butted gun in Jim North's right hand spat its unholy message a part of a second faster than the Frontier Colt of Gideon James.

Jim North was right, some of the gun-magic had helped his hand to incredible speed. The tall blond professional gunman stared and slowly dropped his gun as a red stain appeared on his immaculate shirt – right over his heart.

He fell forward, crashing to the rocks beneath him.

Jim North looked at the pearl-handled gun, turned it over – and then threw it far away among the yellow boulders.

'I'm finished with that hogleg! Me – I don't want a gun with notches …'

The youthful Rod Kane walked on slowly, then stood carefully on his booted feet.

He turned to Jim North. 'Find his hoss. I'm kinda sick of the job, *amigo*.'

He was thinking forward to the weeks and months when the name of Al Smith would mean nothing to a certain girl. And perhaps she would think more kindly of one young deputy…